"If I could undo the past, make up for how I hurt you—"

"Don't say it, Tripp. We're not going there tonight. And never again, okay?" It was the only way Diana could bear being this close to him. "That was then, this is now and all that matters is the people we are today."

In the depths of those intense blue eyes, Diana saw something that rocked her to her core. "If you believe that," he began hesitantly, "then do you think we could start over?"

Her heart stammered. "Start over?"

With a tender smile, Tripp took her hand. "Please. Give me a chance to get it right this time."

"You've got to know how scary this is for me. My heart won't survive getting broken again."

A long, slow sigh escaped Tripp's lips. "As far as it's in my power, I promise that won't happen."

His choice of words struck a subtle warning note in Diana's brain, but she was too caught up in the moment to care.

Award-winning author **Myra Johnson** writes emotionally gripping stories about love, life and faith. She is a two-time finalist for the ACFW Carol Award and winner of the 2005 RWA Golden Heart® Award. Married since 1972, Myra and her husband have two married daughters and seven grandchildren. Although Myra is a native Texan, she and her husband now reside in North Carolina, sharing their home with two pampered rescue dogs.

Books by Myra Johnson

Love Inspired

Hill Country Reunion

Myra Johnson

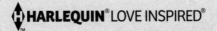

HARLEQUIN® LOVE INSPIRED®

Recycling programs
for this product may
not exist in your area.

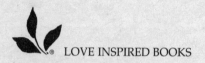

LOVE INSPIRED BOOKS

ISBN-13: 978-1-335-50930-7

Hill Country Reunion

Copyright © 2018 by Myra Johnson

www.Harlequin.com

Printed in U.S.A.

My grace is sufficient for thee:
for my strength is made perfect in weakness.
—*2 Corinthians* 12:9

Remembering all the special pets whose unconditional love has made a difference in my life, and dedicated to the caring veterinarians who have helped to keep our pets healthy.

With thanks once again to my dear friend and Love Inspired Historical author Janet Dean for her insightful advice during the early planning stages of this story. You never fail to get me thinking in new directions!

Chapter One

Saturday mornings at Diana's Donuts typically brought brisk business, but today had gotten just plain ridiculous. Must be the hint of fall in the late-September air, because Diana Matthews couldn't brew coffee fast enough, and the steady flow of customers had all but cleaned out the bakery case.

"Here you go, Alan, a half caf and a blueberry muffin. Sorry we ran out of crullers." With a friendly but frazzled smile, Diana handed Juniper Bluff's local insurance agent his change, then swiveled toward the kitchen. "Kimberly, how are those scones coming?"

"Five more minutes," came her assistant's shout.

A crusty farmer, one of Diana's regulars, plopped his empty coffee mug on the counter. "Di, honey, how about a refill?"

"How many times do I have to tell you, LeRoy? It's *Diana*." Her smile tightened as she poured. She'd never cared much for the nickname—or being called anybody's "honey"—at least not since the person who'd once used such endearments had vanished from her life.

"But, Di, your doughnuts are to *die for*. Get it?" LeRoy laughed at his own play on words.

She widened her grin to disguise an annoyed eye roll.

Her apron pocket vibrated with a call on her cell phone. The display showed her dad's number. "Ethan," she called to the freckled teenager who bused tables on Saturdays, "cover the register for me. I need to take this call."

While Ethan scurried around to help the next customer, Diana slipped into her office. "Hey, Dad, how's it going with Aunt Jennie?"

"All packed and ready to go. We should get to the care center around noon. Any chance you can meet us there?"

Diana's heart warmed in anticipation. Mom and Dad had driven over to San Antonio yesterday to move Dad's aunt into an assisted-living facility on the outskirts of Juniper Bluff. "I'll try, but we're crazy-busy today. On top of everything else, Nora, my part-time counter girl, called in sick."

"Uh-oh. Well, get there when you can. Aunt Jennie's been asking about you, and you know you're her favorite great-niece."

"Yeah, right," Diana said with a chuckle. "Only because I bribe her with cream-filled chocolate doughnuts." She peeked through the miniblinds to see how Ethan was faring. "Give Aunt Jennie my love, and tell her I'll see her real soon."

Clicking off, she hurried out in time to help Ethan fill an order for four lattes to go, along with the last two apple fritters.

"I'll take over here," she said. "Looks like some tables need clearing." As Ethan grabbed a dish tub and cleaning cloth, Diana gave her attention to the next customer.

"Mornin', Diana." Doc Ingram, Juniper Bluff's longtime veterinarian, slid some bills across the counter. "Need two regular coffees and—" he frowned toward the bakery case "—two of whatever you've got left."

"Sorry, we've been swamped today. If you can hang on a sec, Kimberly's about to bring out some fresh-baked cinnamon-raisin scones." Diana reached behind her for two ceramic mugs bearing the pink Diana's Donuts logo. "Who's the other coffee for?" She looked past the doc for a glimpse of his companion.

A familiar face beneath close-cropped brown hair grinned hesitantly back at her. "Hello, Di."

Both mugs crashed to the tile floor. Diana gasped and skittered backward as hot coffee splashed her bare ankles between her sneakers and jeans cuffs.

Kimberly had just stepped through from the kitchen with a tray of scones. "Diana, are you okay?"

"I'm fine." Teeth clenched, eyes lowered, Diana snatched a wet cloth from the workstation and swiped at her legs. No way could she risk another glance at the man standing next to Doc Ingram. It couldn't be. It simply *could not be* Tripp Willoughby.

Kimberly shoved the tray of scones into the display case, then grabbed a broom and dustpan. "You take care of the customers. I'll get this cleaned up."

Murmuring her thanks, Diana bent over the sink to rinse out the coffee-stained cloth, using those few moments to compose herself. After drying her hands, she squared her shoulders and turned. With studied slowness, she let her gaze drift upward to the face of the man she'd never expected to see again.

Concern etched the hard planes of Tripp's features. "Sorry for taking you by surprise like that. Sure you're okay?"

"Of course. My goodness, Tripp, what's it been—ten years? Twelve?" As if she didn't recall the exact day, hour and minute he'd told her it was over between them. Flicking at a wayward strand of hair, trimmed to shoulder length now instead of the waist-long braid she'd worn through college, Diana wondered if she looked as different to him as he did to her.

"Been a while, hasn't it?" At least he had the decency to show a little remorse. Shame-faced guilt would have suited the occasion even better.

One elbow propped on the napkin dispenser, Doc Ingram arched a gray-flecked brow. "What am I missing here? You two know each other?"

"We, um, met in college." With a shaky laugh, Diana edged away. "Let me try again with those coffees."

Kimberly had most of the spill mopped up. Their backs to the customers, she nudged Diana. "Lucy, you got some 'splainin' to do."

"Cool it, Kim. Go bake more muffins or something." After filling two new mugs, Diana carefully set them on the front counter. She smiled stiffly at Tripp. "First coffee and pastry is on the house. Care for one of our fresh-baked scones?"

"Thanks, but I'll stick with just coffee." He scanned the menu board behind Diana's head. "Unless I could have one of those Greek yogurts instead?"

Pursing her lips, she wondered when the guy who used to inhale junk food like it was going out of style decided to eat healthy. "Sure. Plain, berry or lemon?"

"Plain, thanks. Any chance you have soy milk for the coffee?"

"On the condiments bar to your right." Diana retrieved a yogurt from the cooler, then turned her attention to Doc Ingram. "How about a warm, buttery scone for you, Doc—or have you gone health-nut on me, too?"

A bemused look in his eye, the vet quirked a grin. "I'll take two, thanks. Need some carbs to tide me over for my farm calls."

"Great. Y'all find a table and I'll bring your scones right out." Diana took Doc Ingram's payment and handed him a receipt.

When another customer stepped up to the counter, it was all Diana could do to tear her gaze from Tripp's retreating back. She hurriedly filled a coffee order, then snatched two scones from the display case.

Kimberly had just returned from disposing of the shattered mugs. "You're looking a little freaked out. Want me to deliver those?"

"No—actually, yes. I think I'm getting a headache."

"Hope you didn't catch Nora's bug." Kimberly leaned closer and squinted, then wiggled her brows. "Nope, looks more like a bad case of blast-from-the-past blues. I'm warning you, soon as things slow down around here, you are telling me everything you know about our good-looking newcomer."

While Kimberly took the scones out to Doc Ingram's table, Diana made sure the other customers had been served. The steady flow seemed to have tapered off, so she took advantage of the lull to clean up the workstation.

And to eavesdrop. Even with all the other conversations droning around her, she had no trouble homing in on Kimberly's voice as the perky bakery assistant chatted it up with Doc Ingram and Tripp.

"So you're new in town?" Kimberly was saying. "Didn't catch your name."

"Tripp. Tripp Willoughby." His rich baritone was still as silky-smooth as Diana remembered. "Just moved here a couple days ago."

Oh, great. He was *living* in Juniper Bluff now? Stomach flipping, Diana squeezed her eyes shut.

"Tripp's taking over the small-animal side of my practice," Doc Ingram explained. "Now I'll be able to focus entirely on horses and cattle, like I've been hoping to do for a while."

"So it's *Doctor* Willoughby—cool!" Kimberly bubbled. "My little dachshund's about due for her yearly checkup. I'll be sure to make an appointment."

Diana scoured the coffee stains around the sink drain and hoped she hadn't flirted quite so overtly when her former high school classmate Seth Austin would stop in before he and Christina got engaged last year. Now they were happily married and expecting twins.

While Diana remained depressingly single.

Of your own choosing, she reminded herself. She hadn't exactly been dateless since things ended with Tripp, but no relationship since had made it past the superficial level.

She dared a glance across the shop. Kimberly had moved on from Tripp's table to pour coffee refills for other customers. Without other distractions, and without being obvious, Diana could observe the man who'd unceremoniously broken her heart the fall of her senior year in college—and just when she'd been so certain they had something special going on.

Apparently, she'd completely misread Tripp's signals, and everything she'd imagined about sharing a future with him was just that—all in her imagination.

Was it only Tripp's imagination, or was Diana staring a hole through the side of his head? He didn't dare shift his gaze to find out.

He'd sure gotten an eyeful when he'd stepped through the door earlier. Diana Matthews was every bit as beautiful as he remembered. Yep, even without the waist-length dark brown braid he used to love weaving his fingers through. The fresh herbal scent of the shampoo she'd always used still lingered in his memory.

What had he gone and done, accepting Robert Ingram's offer of a partnership in his veterinary practice—and when Tripp *knew* Juniper Bluff was Diana's hometown?

Okay, so he'd wrongly assumed Diana would be married, with 2.5 kids and living somewhere far, far away from here by now. Hadn't his sister told him only a few months after the breakup that Diana was seeing someone else?

Besides, he couldn't pass up this opportunity to get out of the big city and leave behind the pressures of a huge practice where he was one of fourteen vets on staff and rarely got to see the same patient twice in a row.

"Coffee okay?" Robert's question, laced with friendly concern, interrupted Tripp's thoughts.

"Yeah. Fine." Not the coffee fanatic he used to be, he stirred in another splash of soy milk and hoped his stomach would settle quickly.

"Had no idea you knew Diana. Small world, huh?"

"Yeah."

Robert polished off the last two bites of his scones, then drained his coffee mug. "Need anything else before we head back to the clinic?"

"I'm good, thanks." Pushing back his chair, Tripp avoided so much as a glance in Diana's direction, scared to death of what he'd see in her eyes. After how he'd left things, she had every right to despise him.

He'd just hoped, after all these years, she might have forgiven and forgotten.

Like he could ever forget her. Or forgive himself.

Outside, he inhaled a bolstering breath of sun-warmed Texas air and followed Robert to the white dually pickup with Ingram Veterinary Hospital and the clinic phone number emblazoned across both sides.

As they neared the clinic on the south edge of town, Robert broke the silence that had settled between them. "Ready to hold down the fort while I head out on some calls?"

"No problem." Tripp mentally reviewed the small-animal appointments scheduled for the rest of the morning. It should be a slow and easy first day on the job.

Robert pulled in behind the long, gray-brick clinic building and shut off the engine. He angled Tripp a curious grin. "You always this talkative?"

With a self-conscious chuckle, Tripp shook his head. "Guess I'm still recovering from the shock of running into Diana."

"I'm getting the impression y'all were way more than just college friends."

"Yeah." Tripp sighed. "We were."

"Well, she's still single, and so are you, right?" Quirking a grin, Robert shoved open his door. "And

Diana's Donuts is the best place in town to get your morning cup of java."

Tripp sat in the pickup a moment longer while his new partner's words sank in. Could it be more than mere coincidence that had landed him in Juniper Bluff? Was this God's way of fixing the worst mistake Tripp had ever made in his crazy, mixed-up life?

Noticing Robert already had the back door to the clinic unlocked, Tripp scrambled from the pickup. Not a good idea to flake out on his first day. While Robert geared up for his farm calls, Tripp grabbed a lab coat on his way to check in with Yolanda, the salt-and-pepper-haired receptionist.

"Good, you're back." Yolanda nodded to the waiting area. "Mrs. Cox just got here for her ten a.m. appointment—Schatzi's annual checkup and shots. Plus, we've got two walk-ins. Sue Ellen Jamison's cat needs to be dewormed, and Carl Vasquez's German shepherd tangled with a coyote last night."

Tripp smiled toward the pet owners. "Bring Mr. Vasquez and his dog to exam room one. Apologize to Mrs. Cox for the delay, and tell Ms. Jamison we'll work her in as soon as we can."

Two hectic but gratifying hours later, he scanned the empty waiting area. Yes—all caught up, and none too soon. It was lunchtime, and his stomach was growling louder than Sue Ellen Jamison's angry cat.

"I heard that," Yolanda said with a snicker. She made a notation in a patient file, then tucked it into a slot on the shelf behind her. "By the way, Sue Ellen said to tell you nobody's ever gotten Cleopatra to take her medicine as easily as you did."

Tripp rubbed the teeth marks on his left thumb. "Then I'd hate to see the last vet who tried."

"That would be Doc Ingram, and he has the scars to prove it." Yolanda shut down the computer, scooped up her shoulder bag and started turning off lights. "Truth is, I think Cleopatra had a whole lot to do with convincing the doc it was time to bring a small-animal vet on board."

"Well, there was no mention of a psychopathic Siamese in the paperwork I signed." Chuckling, Tripp followed the receptionist out the rear door. They said their goodbyes, and Tripp climbed into his SUV. Time to grab a sandwich and some groceries and head home.

With only a couple of days between his last day at his former practice and coming to Juniper Bluff, Tripp hadn't had much time to settle in. Robert Ingram had made arrangements for Tripp to stay at a place outside of town called Serenity Hills Guest Ranch. One of their staff cabins was currently vacant, and for a bachelor like Tripp, the single bedroom, small living area and kitchenette would serve him just fine until either the owners kicked him out or he found a place closer to the clinic.

As he waited for his to-go order at the supermarket deli, another advantage of living so far out of town occurred to him: a much smaller likelihood of accidentally running into Diana. Despite what Robert had hinted about the possibility of their getting back together, Tripp figured he'd long ago blown his chances.

Anyway, hadn't he pretty much convinced himself marriage and family weren't for him? Something much more ominous than hunger pangs could be blamed for the rumblings in his abdomen. Sure, the Crohn's might be well controlled most of the time, but flare-ups were inevitable. And how, in good conscience, could Tripp ever risk passing on this possibly genetic and sometimes excruciatingly painful disease to any children in his future?

Business at the doughnut shop generally slowed as lunchtime approached, which meant Diana could turn things over to Kimberly and get away for a while. Still shaken by the unexpected encounter with Tripp, she needed a break before her runaway emotions got the best of her—*and* before her nosy assistant had a chance to pepper her with more questions.

Figuring her parents would be too busy helping Aunt Jennie move in to think about lunch, she filled a small white bag with her great-aunt's favorite doughnuts, then texted her mom with an offer to run by the supermarket deli and pick up sandwiches.

At the supermarket, a line of customers waited at the deli counter, so she picked up a sandwich menu and joined the queue.

While she studied the menu, someone paused beside her. "I hear the ham-and-Swiss is really good."

The page nearly fell from her hand. "Tripp."

"Yep, it's still me." His lopsided grin made her stomach dip. He held up a bulging deli bag. "Guess great minds think alike."

Or not. Diana forced a smile. "Just moved in and you're already discovering all the popular eateries in Juniper Bluff. When you're ready to try Mexican, I recommend Casa Luis."

An odd look crossed Tripp's face. "Thanks, I'll keep it in mind."

"Oh, I forgot. You're on some kind of health kick these days."

"You could say so." Tripp glanced away. "Well, don't let me keep you. Have a good afternoon, Diana."

"Yeah, you, too." The line moved, and Diana took a giant step forward. She was so ready to end this conversation.

"Diana?"

She winced, then turned and met Tripp's steady gaze. "Yes?"

"I just wanted to say how good it is to see you again. Your own business and everything—that's…really great. I'm happy for you."

At the pensive look in his eyes, the corner of her heart that had been frozen all these years melted a tiny bit. "Thanks. I'm glad to know you're doing well, too. I hope you'll be very happy in Juniper Bluff."

"I think I will be. The slower pace is already a welcome change."

"Funny," Diana mused with a twist to her lips, "I didn't think anything could lure you from your big-city lifestyle."

Tripp shrugged. "Maybe that was true…once."

"Well, I guess a lot can change in twelve years."

"Yeah, a lot can change." The words came out on a sigh. After a moment's pause, he offered a parting smile and strode away.

Lost in trying to figure out what this new Tripp Willoughby was all about, Diana jumped when the deli clerk called her name. "Oh, hi, Stan. Yes, I'd like two Reubens, an egg salad on whole wheat and a ham-and-Swiss on rye, light on the mustard."

She added a gallon of fresh-brewed iced tea to her

order, then selected a large bag of chips. Fifteen minutes later, she was on her way to the assisted-living center.

By the time she arrived, she'd regained a semblance of composure. At the reception desk she asked for directions to Aunt Jennie's quarters, then followed the signs to apartment 18C. The door stood open, and her great-aunt beamed from the opposite end of a small dinette.

Aunt Jennie stretched out her arms. "Come around here and give me a big ol' hug!"

Diana dropped the deli and doughnut bags onto the table, then scooped the petite ninety-two-year-old into a gentle but enthusiastic embrace. "I'm so glad you're finally here!"

Aunt Jennie patted Diana's cheek as she knelt on the carpet beside her chair. In a conspiratorial whisper, she asked, "Did you remember my favorite doughnuts?"

"Right here." Diana slid the smallest bag closer. Rising, she swept her gaze around the room. "Oh, good, you brought some of your own things to make it feel more like home."

"Yes, but it was very sad leaving my comfy little house and garden." The elderly woman's lips turned down with remorse. "Even harder to give up my sweet little Ginger-dog."

"I know, and I'm so sorry." Diana had known Aunt Jennie wouldn't be allowed to bring her lovable corgi to the new apartment. Aunt Jennie's next-door neighbor Mrs. Doudtman had taken Ginger, saying she'd be a great playmate for her two shelties.

"She'll adjust, honey, just like I will." Aunt Jennie patted Diana's arm.

Her great-aunt might be putting up a brave front, but the wistful look in her eyes every time she mentioned

Ginger's name brought a lump to Diana's throat. She'd have offered to keep Ginger herself, but she already shared her two-bedroom cottage with three cats, a lop-eared rabbit and a parakeet. Besides, her tiny backyard wasn't fenced, so a dog was out of the question. Ginger was too prissy to last long as a farm dog, which meant Diana's parents weren't able to take her, either.

But Diana did have an idea she hoped to implement soon. She'd begun investigating programs where volunteers brought pets to visit shut-ins, and if things worked out, she planned to establish a group right here in Juniper Bluff.

Thinking about pets brought to mind an unexpected complication. Unless Diana wanted to drive the extra miles to a veterinary clinic in a neighboring town, anytime her menagerie needed health care, she'd have no choice but to make an appointment with Tripp.

Chapter Two

Nothing like fresh country air to sweep away the mental cobwebs. A plate of scrambled eggs and toast in one hand, a glass of almond milk in the other, Tripp eased into a red retro-style metal lawn chair and propped one bare foot on the porch rail. He couldn't ask for a more relaxing start to a Sunday morning.

For now, at least, it remained quiet. Not long after he'd arrived to start moving in on Friday, Serenity Hills Guest Ranch was invaded by a vanload of excited kids. Tripp's landlord, Seth Austin, had apologized for not giving him a heads-up about Camp Serenity, a program the ranch participated in for disadvantaged children. Turned out this was one of their camping weekends.

The clop-clop of horses' hooves drew Tripp's attention to the tree-shaded lane. Moments later Seth Austin ambled into view with his towheaded young son, Joseph, each of them leading a horse.

"Mornin'." While his son continued on, Seth halted in front of Tripp's cabin. "Getting settled in okay?"

Tripp swallowed a bite of toast before replying. "Close. Got a few more things to unpack."

"Any problems, feel free to holler." Seth patted his horse's neck. "Just taking horses out to pasture. Didn't mean to disturb you."

"Not at all. I grew up in the city, but my grandparents used to have horses. Nice being around them again."

"Anytime you're up for a trail ride, I'm happy to oblige. In fact," Seth said with a nod behind him toward the barn, "we'll be taking several campers out for one more ride this afternoon before they head back to San Antonio. You're welcome to come along."

"Thanks, I'll think about it."

"Oh, and my wife and kids are going into town for Sunday school and church this morning. Christina would be happy to introduce you around."

Tripp chewed his lip. Juniper Bluff was a small town. How likely was it that Diana went to the same church? Nope, not quite ready to risk running into her again. "Maybe next time, after I get a little more organized."

"Sure thing." Seth clucked to his horse and continued along the lane. "Let me know if you're interested in that trail ride."

"I will. Thanks."

While Tripp finished breakfast, the nickering of horses, birdcalls from the treetops and the scent of cedar in the air lulled him into the deepest sense of relaxation he'd felt since before he started veterinary school. Man, did he need this! After a couple of debilitating flare-ups within the last several months, his doctor had warned him that if he didn't significantly reduce his stress level, keeping the Crohn's under control would be next to impossible.

From beyond the trees came the sounds of doors banging and children's laughter. The campers must be up and about. Tripp took the commotion as his cue to go inside.

As he set his breakfast dishes in the sink, his cell phone rang. The display showed his little sister, Brooke's name and number. "Hey, sis."

"Hey, yourself. All moved in yet?" Much more a morning person than Tripp would ever be, she sounded way too perky for 6 a.m. California time.

"Getting there. How's it going with Mom?"

Brooke's long sigh drained all the lightness from her tone. "Not so good, Tripp. She's trying hard to be positive, but the dialysis routine is wearing her down."

Tripp sank into the nearest chair and massaged his eye sockets. Fighting kidney disease for the past few years, their mom seemed closer than ever to losing the battle. "How's Dad handling it?"

"He's struggling. Yesterday I caught him behind the garage crying his eyes out."

The image of his father breaking down brought a catch to Tripp's throat. "I'm glad they moved out there with you, but I feel bad I can't be of more help." As the only family member who'd tested close enough to be a potential match for kidney donation, he felt even worse. The Crohn's made him ineligible. "Maybe I should have transferred to a vet clinic near you in Los Angeles instead of staying here in Texas."

"No, Tripp, you'd hate it here. I would never have relocated to LA if not for Jeff—and then right when I thought the jerk was about to propose—" A gulp left the rest of her statement unspoken. "Tripp, I'm sorry. Our situations were totally different."

"It's okay. I get it." But he could have done without

the reminder of how he'd ended things with Diana. Best to change the subject. "You still like your job, right?"

"Definitely." A smile had returned to her voice. "Getting promoted to accounts manager for an advertising firm has been my dream since college. So whenever I start fixating on…other things…I remind myself of the story of Joseph in the Bible where he tells his brothers, 'You intended to harm me, but God intended it for good.'" Her tone softened. "You need to believe that, too."

"Yeah, most days I try." The thing was, Tripp had never wanted to hurt Diana, not in a million years. His Crohn's diagnosis had hit him hard, though, and he felt he had to come to grips with it on his own before even considering bringing that kind of baggage into a relationship. During those difficult early months of two steps forward, one step back, as he learned to live with the disease, he'd convinced himself he'd done Diana a kindness by letting her go.

"Hey, bro, I really called to find out how you're doing. Do you like the new clinic?"

"Nice people, a lot less stress. I think it'll be a good fit." *Except for one tiny detail.* "Uh, Brooke?" Back to the subject he didn't seem able to avoid. "Did you happen to remember Juniper Bluff is where Diana Matthews is from?"

"Diana—oh, wow! It's been so long I'd forgotten." A concerned pause hung between them. "Does she still live there? Have you seen her?"

"Yes, and yes. She runs her own bakery and coffee shop, Diana's Donuts. My new partner took me there for coffee yesterday."

"Yikes. Was it ridiculously awkward?"

"You could say so." Their second encounter at the supermarket deli hadn't been much easier.

"Maybe this is your chance to clear the air. I still can't believe you never told her *why* you ended things. Do you have any idea how hard it was for me to keep your secret?"

"I know. It wasn't fair." He plowed his fingers through his hair. "But she's got her own life now. After all this time, what if telling her the truth only hurts her more?"

"Or…what if it gives you two a chance to fall in love all over again?"

Tripp hadn't so much as hinted that Diana was still single, and now he wasn't about to. Seemed like the perfect time to end the call, before his sister went any more hopelessly romantic on him. "How about you tend to your own love life and let me tend to mine." Dismal as it was. "Bye, sis. Give Mom and Dad hugs for me."

Later, as he arranged socks and T-shirts in the chest of drawers, his hand grazed the small velveteen box he'd never been able to part with, its contents an ever-present reminder of what he'd given up. He opened the lid for one more longing look at the classically elegant diamond ring nestled inside, while his sister's parting words played through his mind. What if he and Diana really could find their way back to each other?

And how many more regrets would he carry through life if he didn't try?

Closing the shop after the early Sunday morning coffee-and-doughnuts rush, Diana almost decided to skip church. Why risk running into Tripp again in case he tagged along with Doc Ingram?

But the past was the past, and she was a big girl now. Anyway, Juniper Bluff was too small a town to avoid Tripp for long—seeing him twice in the same day had proven as much—and she refused to rearrange her life on his account.

Even so, when Doc Ingram and his wife arrived without Tripp in tow, Diana relaxed slightly. She offered a friendly nod but couldn't help wondering how much Tripp had revealed about their shared history.

Leaving the sanctuary after worship, Diana spotted Christina Austin, pregnant with twins and already showing. Her service dog, Gracie, stood faithfully at her side. The gentle golden retriever, who helped Christina deal with the aftereffects of the traumatic brain injury she'd suffered in a car accident a few years ago, reminded Diana yet again how an animal's love and devotion could make a positive difference in someone's life.

She ambled over to say hello. "Hey, lady, how are things at the ranch?"

Christina turned with a cheery smile. She held the hand of her seven-year-old stepdaughter, Eva. "It's another Camp Serenity weekend. Need I say more?"

"Ah. That explains your handsome hubby's absence. Did Joseph stay home, too?"

"No, he's around here somewhere." Christina's glance swept the crowded foyer. "He had a question about his pony for Doc Ingram."

Eva looped one arm around Gracie's neck. "I have a pony now, too," she told Diana. "Her name's Candy."

"Wow, that's great!" Diana knelt to tweak Eva's pale yellow curls. "Can I come see her sometime?"

"Sure. We're gonna do a trail ride with the campers after lunch. Wanna come with us?"

Diana hadn't had much time lately to take her own horse out on the trail, and the weather today would be perfect. She pushed to her feet. "What time are y'all heading out?"

"They'll saddle up around one thirty," Christina replied. "Seth can always use an extra hand to keep those energetic campers in line." She patted her pregnant belly. "And I'm not much help these days, especially if it involves getting on a horse."

"It does sound fun." Diana checked her watch. She could easily grab a bite for lunch, run out to her parents' ranch to load Mona in the horse trailer and make it out to Serenity Hills in time for the ride. "Okay, count me in."

By one o'clock she'd stowed her saddle and other gear in the tack compartment of her dad's one-horse trailer, already hitched to his pickup. Mona, her copper penny bay mare, looked eager for a change of scenery and pranced into the trailer with her head held high.

"Hope you settle down before we get there," Diana said as she clipped the trailer tie to Mona's halter. "I don't need any extra drama this weekend." Seeing Tripp Willoughby walk into her doughnut shop yesterday was about all the drama she could handle for the next, oh, fifty years or so.

At Serenity Hills, Seth Austin and his stable hands already had several horses saddled and tied to the corral fence. Waving to him as she passed, Diana pulled into a parking area next to the barn.

As she stepped around to the rear of the horse trailer, Seth ambled over and offered a friendly hug. "Christina said you'd probably join us. Need some help with Mona?"

"I'm fine." Diana grinned toward the camp counselors struggling to buckle riding helmets onto the heads of several rambunctious campers. "Anyway, looks like you've got your hands full over there."

"That's the truth. Two more hours and we'll have peace and quiet again." Seth exaggerated a look of fatigue, but Diana knew how much he enjoyed the arrangement he and his grandparents, Bryan and Marie Peterson, had made with the San Antonio–based philanthropic organization that sponsored Camp Serenity. Besides saving the family from having to sell the guest ranch, the camp provided fun and adventure for kids who might otherwise never have the chance to get out of the city, much less to learn about horses and riding.

Diana unlatched the trailer door, and Seth gave her a hand lowering the ramp. Sidling into the trailer, Diana clipped a lead rope to Mona's halter and prepared to back her down the ramp. Apparently, the drive over had only heightened the mare's excitement. "Easy, girl."

"She's lookin' kind of feisty." Seth laid a steadying hand on Mona's rump.

"No kidding." Diana barely got her toe out of the way in time to keep from getting stomped on. "Maybe I'll take her over to the round pen and see if I can settle her down some."

Seth returned to his campers while Diana walked Mona to the round pen. Standing in the center of the fifty-foot-diameter pen, Diana used a lunge whip to send her horse into a trot around the perimeter. When Mona began to settle down after a few circuits, Diana wasn't quite so concerned about getting tossed on her keister somewhere out on the trail.

At the horse trailer, she buckled on Mona's saddle

and bridle and mounted up as Seth started her way leading his trail riders. Immediately behind him were Joseph on Spot and Eva riding her new palomino pony.

One hand gripping the reins and saddle horn, the little girl grinned and waved. "Hey, Miss Diana! You came!"

"Sure did, hon. Is this Candy? She's adorable!"

Eva beamed. "You can ride next to me, okay?"

"Love to." Diana prepared to fall in step.

Then, as she glanced back toward the other riders in the lineup, a familiar pair of crystal-blue eyes locked gazes with her—*Tripp*.

She froze, her jaw going slack, while Tripp Willoughby drew closer and closer.

"Miss Diana," Eva called, "hurry and catch up."

She snapped her mouth shut. Nudging Mona with her boot heels, she reined the horse around and trotted up next to Eva. When she could find her voice, she said, "Hey, Seth, what's with the, um, new volunteer?"

Straining to look past her over his shoulder, Seth grinned. "Oh, you mean Doc Ingram's new partner? He's just along for the ride. We're renting him one of the staff cabins."

"So he's…he's living *here*?" Her voice climbed an octave. "On your ranch?"

"Yep. Sorry I didn't get a chance to introduce you. Remind me when we get back later."

Diana grimaced. "That's okay. We've already met."

Diana was riding with them? Great. And Tripp assumed living out at Serenity Hills would mean fewer unexpected encounters with the woman he'd never gotten out of his heart.

Could this move to Juniper Bluff get any more complicated?

Maybe if he made sure to stay at the rear of the line, he could spare them both more discomfort.

And yet…man, she looked good on the back of a horse! He'd seen Diana in boots and jeans plenty of times, even gone riding with her when they used to spend weekends now and then at his grandparents' place outside Austin. The passage of time had only made her more beautiful, and though he did miss the long hair, her shorter, perkier ponytail poking out beneath a tan felt Stetson added a certain amount of sass.

Not that she didn't have plenty already. The look she'd shot him a few moments ago was one hundred percent sass. Although in that split second of recognition, Tripp had definitely glimpsed something else in her expression, and it looked a whole lot like panic. Considering he'd had the same reaction to their third unplanned meeting in less than two days, he ought to know.

Noticing his poky old cow horse was falling behind, he gave the beast a gentle kick. "Git up, Tex. No backing out now. Might as well see this through."

The trail meandered past a small lake and picnic area, then up a rocky slope shaded by cedars and live oaks. The hills should have been teeming with birds and animals, but with the campers laughing and howling like wild animals themselves, any expectations Tripp had about observing wildlife soon vanished.

He was too busy watching Diana anyway. And making sure to keep a nice, safe distance between them. Once or twice on the way up the hillside, she scrunched up her shoulders as if she could feel his eyes on her, but she never looked back.

Soon the trail opened into a meadow tufted with brown grass. Up ahead, Seth angled right, leading the riders in a wide circle as they changed directions for the return to the barn. In another few strides, Diana would be riding directly toward Tripp. His pulse ratcheted up a good twenty beats per minute. Would she say anything? Would she even look at him?

"Hi, Tripp." She spoke. Even smiled. At least he thought so. With her face shaded by the hat and a pair of sporty sunglasses, it was hard to be sure. "Enjoying the ride?"

He had about three seconds before their paths would diverge. "Yeah, can't beat this weather."

"Mmm-hmm." The quirk of her mouth told him exactly how lame his reply had sounded.

When she rode on by and he was once again bringing up the rear, he let out a frustrated sigh. Brooke was right—eventually he needed to be honest with Diana about why he'd broken things off. Maybe if she knew the truth, she'd forgive him.

If only he could count on forgiveness being her *only* response. The whole point of *not* telling her in the first place was so she wouldn't stick by him out of pity or obligation. If they did have any chance of starting over—if Diana would even give him the time of day after how he'd hurt her—he wasn't about to risk a "sympathy relationship" by playing the Crohn's card.

Up ahead, a flicker of motion caught Tripp's eye—a startled deer bounding into the woods. In the same instant, Diana's horse shied and skittered sideways. Tripp swallowed a gasp as Diana landed hard in a clump of dry grass.

"Hold up, everyone," Seth shouted as he wheeled

his horse around. He instructed those nearest Diana to move their horses a safe distance away.

Tripp wasn't waiting. He urged Tex forward, swinging out of the saddle the moment he drew even with Diana. He knelt beside her, resisting the impulse to physically check her for broken bones. "You okay?"

"Stupid horse. I knew she was way too full of herself." Diana sat up and rubbed her hip, then groaned as she snatched up her mangled sunglasses. "There goes fifty bucks down the drain."

Tripp couldn't care less about the glasses. "Take it slow. You might be hurt worse than you think."

"Stop looking at me like I'm one of your patients." Diana's hat lay an arm's reach away. She slapped it onto her head, then cautiously pushed to her feet. Brushing dead grass off her jeans, she scowled at Tripp. "I'm fine, I promise. The worst damage is to my ego."

Seth rode over, leading Diana's horse. "Here you go." He snickered as he handed her the reins. "Guess y'all should have taken a little longer in the round pen."

"Guess *you* should keep your opinions to yourself, cowboy." Diana's sharp tone didn't match the teasing twinkle in her eye, which reassured Tripp she really was unhurt.

Her horse still looked a little skittish, so Tripp kept a firm grip on the mare's bridle while Diana climbed into the saddle. Once she'd settled, he looked around for his own mount. Tex hadn't wandered far, seeming content to munch on grass and ignore the commotion. Back in the saddle, Tripp decided he'd risk Diana's scorn and ride next to her in case her horse acted up again.

By then, the other riders had continued on, leaving

Tripp and Diana at the back of the line. Exhaling loudly, she glanced over. "Thanks for coming to my rescue."

He cocked his head and grinned. "Yeah, it brought back memories."

"Oh, please. Don't you dare bring up the time at your grandparents' when my horse threw me into the water trough."

At least she was smiling—a good sign. "That had to be a softer landing than today."

"No kidding. My hip's going to be a zillion shades of purple by this time tomorrow." Diana sat straighter and cleared her throat. "We should catch up with the others. I still need to go visit my aunt this afternoon."

"Aunt Jennie's in town?"

She looked surprised he'd remembered the great-aunt she'd always been so fond of. "Yes, as of yesterday." Briefly, Diana told him about moving Aunt Jennie into the assisted-living center. "I'm just sorry she had to give up her dog. Juniper Bluff really needs a therapy pets program."

"If you need help starting one—"

"Got it covered." Diana clucked to her horse. "Let's go, Mona. We're getting left behind."

Then Tripp was the one left behind, since the old trail horse was content to plod along at a snail's pace. Just when he thought things were relaxing between him and Diana, she'd shut him down. Was there any hope at all they could come through this as friends?

Was he crazy to hope for more?

Chapter Three

Returning to the barn after the ride, Tripp clipped Tex to the cross ties at the far end of the barn aisle and loosened the saddle cinch.

Seth moved down the line to check on the campers, then stopped next to Tripp. "So you and Diana know each other?"

"Small world, huh?" Tripp managed a quick laugh. "She and my sister were college roomies." It was the truth. Just not all of it.

Hiking a brow, Seth tipped back his Stetson. "Yeah, that totally explains why you two are walking on eggshells around each other."

"This goes in the tack room, right?" Tripp hefted the heavy saddle off Tex's back.

"I'll take care of it." With a nod toward the barn door, Seth cast Tripp a knowing grin. "She's limping a bit after that fall, so I'm sure she'd appreciate some help with her horse."

Shoulders slumping, Tripp handed over the saddle. The sooner he and Diana could put this awkward phase behind them, the better. Squinting against the afternoon sun, he traipsed out of the barn, hauled in a deep breath and headed for Diana's trailer.

She'd just gotten the horse loaded and grimaced as she stepped off the ramp, clearly favoring her bruised hip.

Tripp hurried over. "Here, let me give you a hand."

"That's okay, I've got it." Turning, she bent to lift the ramp, then groaned beneath the weight.

"Sure you do." Ignoring her refusal, Tripp donated his muscles to the cause. Together they hoisted the ramp into position and secured the latches.

Diana stepped back, dusting off her hands. "Thanks. Again."

"My pleasure." Tripp shifted his stance. "Look, Di—"

"I prefer Diana, if you don't mind."

"Sorry. *Diana*." She wasn't about to make this any easier. "It's pretty clear my being here is making you uncomfortable, and I just wanted to say I'm sorry. If I'd known you were still in Juniper Bluff—"

"What? You'd have turned down Doc Ingram's partnership?" Her withering stare made him flinch. "Yes, this is a small town, but it's plenty big for both of us."

He bristled. "I'm trying to apologize. We were having a nice conversation for a few minutes there on the trail, and I was hoping—"

"That we could be friends? Let bygones be bygones?" Diana brushed past him and marched around to the driver's side of the pickup. "Sure, Tripp," she called over her shoulder. "Don't even think twice about it. It's all in the past."

Catching up, Tripp blocked her from opening the door. "First of all, quit finishing my sentences for me.

Second, I get it. I hurt you, and I'll regret it to my dying day. Third, yes, I would like it very much if we could start over as friends." He let out a long, slow sigh and hoped his desperate half smile would win her over. "Please."

Her throat shifted. She crossed her arms. "You're right," she murmured, "and I'm sorry. I don't like this tension between us any better than you do."

"Thank you." A part of him really, *really* wanted to take her in his arms for a hug, but he figured that might be pushing things. Besides, he was afraid once he held her again, he'd never be able to let go.

She didn't give him the chance anyway. After tossing her hat across to the other seat, she jumped in behind the steering wheel. "Need to get going. See you around."

"Yeah." Tripp stepped back as she yanked the door closed. "See you around."

Diana could not leave Serenity Hills quickly enough. And there was nothing the least bit *serene* about her departure. She could see Tripp sincerely felt bad about barging back into her life. But *friendship*, after she'd thought they were on the verge of making a lifetime commitment? The fact that it still hurt so much only proved the depth of the feelings she once had for him.

Once? All right, *still*. Every man she'd dated since had the misfortune of being held to the standard set by Tripp Willoughby. Either the guy wasn't funny, smart, kind or romantic enough, or if he happened to meet all those criteria, there remained the chance he'd dump Diana just like Tripp had. It was a lose-lose proposition any way she looked at it.

Arriving at her dad's ranch, she returned Mona to

the pasture, then backed the horse trailer into its spot next to the garage. Before she could get it unhitched, her dad came out to help.

"Have a good time?" he asked.

"It was fun—until Mona spooked and I hit the ground."

"Uh-oh. You okay?"

"I'll live." Stooped over the trailer hitch, she could pretend her hip was the only thing bothering her.

When they'd moved the trailer tongue onto a cinder block, she thanked her dad and forestalled more questions by saying she needed to get home and change before going over to see Aunt Jennie. She just hoped to have her emotions a little more under control by then.

An hour later, with freshly washed, finger-combed hair and wearing a clean pair of jeans with a purple peasant top, Diana tapped on the door of her great-aunt's tiny apartment. A soft "Coming, dear" and shuffling feet preceded the click of the doorknob. The door swung open, and Aunt Jennie welcomed Diana with a cheery smile and a warm hug.

Diana stepped into the cozy sitting room. Her great-aunt's plush blue recliner and favorite antique end table added a homey touch. "Looks like Mom and Dad got you all settled. It's a lovely apartment."

"Yes, it's quite comfortable, and the people here are as nice as can be." Aunt Jennie sighed as she eased into the recliner. "Only one thing could make it better."

"I know—you miss Ginger. Tell you what," Diana said as she plopped onto the love seat. "One day this week I'll take you over to my house and you can hug on my critters."

"Oh, that would be wonderful." A bright smile lit

Aunt Jennie's face. "Do you still have all three of those spoiled-rotten cats? And the rabbit, too?"

"Sure do. Plus a stray parakeet I found fluttering around the bird feeder last spring. He's made himself right at home, and he knows how to show those cats who's boss."

As Diana described her menagerie, she itched to get rolling with her plans for a therapy pets program. Not only would it make Aunt Jennie's transition a little easier, but pet visits could bring a spark of life and laughter to the other residents, as well.

The next morning, Diana awoke to a blaring clock radio and an overweight gray-striped tabby sitting on her chest. She slapped the off button on the radio while shoving the cat to one side. "Okay, okay, Tiger, I'm awake."

Midnight and Lucinda, the tomcat's partners in crime, paced across Diana's feet, all apparently near starvation, if their plaintive mews could be believed.

The hardest part of owning a doughnut shop? The 4:00 a.m. wake-up call. And Diana had stayed up entirely too late last night downloading information and application forms for starting a therapy pets program. Tossing back the covers, she stumbled to the bathroom and splashed water on her face, then saw to her pets before sitting down to her own breakfast.

By 4:50 she was out the door. At the shop, she helped Kimberly start batches of doughnuts, muffins, scones and apple fritters, then set up the coffeemakers. At one minute before six, she flipped the Closed sign to Open and unlocked the door.

After the early-morning rush ended, she helped Kimberly get more pastries in the oven, then made herself a café mocha latte and carried it to her office. Logging in to her email account, she hoped to have a response from the therapy pet organization she'd contacted about sponsoring a chapter in Juniper Bluff.

And she did. Agnes Kraus, a representative from Visiting Pet Pals, asked Diana to call at her earliest convenience. Adrenaline pumping, she dialed the number immediately.

"Yes, Diana, it's good to hear from you," Mrs. Kraus said. "We're delighted you want to launch a program in Juniper Bluff." Papers rustled. "I'm looking at your application right now. I see you want to focus on dog owners initially. How are you doing with potential volunteers?"

Diana chewed her lip. "No commitments yet, but I have some acquaintances in mind. I was planning to get going on that over the next few days."

"You do understand each dog must have basic obedience certification? Plus, we require a minimum of eight sign-ups before I can make the trip to evaluate the animals and conduct a training session specific to therapy pets."

"Yes, ma'am," Diana said, quickly jotting reminders. "I have your list of requirements right here in front of me. Once I have my volunteers, how soon could we be evaluated?"

Mrs. Kraus paused, the sound of clicking computer keys filling the silence. "My fall schedule is filling up, so the earliest date would be the second Saturday of November. That would give you about six weeks to get your team together."

Diana clicked open her own calendar and counted

off the weeks. She'd hoped to hold the first official pet visit at the assisted-living center as a surprise for Aunt Jennie's birthday, a few days before Thanksgiving. It just might be doable—provided she could come up with eight qualified dog owners.

"Pencil me in," she told Mrs. Kraus. "I'll do everything possible to be ready by then."

She'd just hung up when Kimberly tapped on the door. "Diana, you might want to see this."

Diana pushed back her chair and stood. "Please don't tell me the oven conked out again."

"No, the oven's working like a champ. It's…something else." Kimberly led the way out to the alley and over to the Dumpster. She pointed into the shadows. "See back there by the wall?"

Muted whimpers wrenched Diana's heart moments before she glimpsed the scrawny mother cat and four newborn kittens nestled inside a crumbling cardboard box. "Oh, dear, you poor things!"

"We can't leave them back there," Kimberly said. "This is trash pickup day. They could be crushed."

Diana edged away, afraid of frightening the cat into running off somewhere even less safe. "Can you keep an eye on things while I run over to the supermarket for some cat food? Maybe I can lure her out and then…" She shrugged. "I'll figure out something."

Half an hour later, Tiger's favorite Shrimp-and-Salmon Delight had the mama cat's nose working overtime. Within five minutes, Diana had made a new friend. While mama dined, Diana and Kimberly transferred the kittens from their dingy hiding place into a sturdier, towel-lined crate. The mama cat climbed in with her kittens, and Diana carried them to her office.

When she checked on them later, snuggled in their box next to the filing cabinet and emitting soft, rumbling purrs, she realized she was already growing attached.

Kimberly peeked in. "How's the little family?"

Diana leaned down to scratch the mama cat behind the ears. "Fine for now, but they can't stay here, and there's no way I can take them home with me." She looked hopefully at her assistant. "Any chance—"

"Uh-uh, no way!" Kimberly held up both hands. "Olivia despises cats."

"Yeah, I forgot." The little dachshund definitely was not cat-friendly.

"Doc Ingram's new partner seems really nice. Maybe he could help find them a home."

Diana's lips flattened. She'd already let that idea zip right on past. Too bad it was the only one that made sense. Juniper Bluff wasn't big enough to have its own animal shelter—the nearest one was over in Fredericksburg— and even so, Diana had no confidence they could find a home for a scrawny mother cat with kittens.

"Okay, Ms. Matthews, no more stalling." Pulling a side chair closer, Kimberly plopped down directly in front of Diana. "What are you not telling me about our handsome new small-animal vet?"

Breath catching in her throat, Diana tipped forward, head in her hands. She was *so* not ready to relive the worst day of her life.

Kimberly set her hand on Diana's shoulder. "Honey, tell me! Did that guy hurt you somehow?"

Heaving a sigh, Diana straightened. "If effectively ripping out my heart, stomping on it with combat boots and dousing it in hydrochloric acid counts, then yes, he hurt me really, really bad."

Kimberly's mouth fell open. "When? How?"

Steeling herself, Diana gave her assistant a condensed version of the facts—how her college apartment mate Brooke Willoughby had invited her along on a weekend visit home to Austin. There, she met Brooke's older brother, Tripp, a veterinary student at Texas A&M. The attraction was immediate, and the more time they spent together, the deeper in love Diana had fallen.

Until the phone call that ended it all. Tripp had caught her between classes—called her cell phone, of all things! The jerk didn't even have the nerve to break it to her in person.

I'm sorry, Di, but...I need to cancel our plans for this weekend.

Tripp, I'm on my way to an economics test. Can I call you back in an hour?

He'd paused too long, a warning in itself. *I need to say this now. About us. This...* A pained swallow. *It's just not working.*

Not working? Her heart had turned stone-cold with dread. *What are you telling me?*

I think we need to slow down a bit, maybe take a break. I'm under a lot of pressure with my vet studies and...other things. It's...complicated.

"I thought he cared for me the same way," Diana said, brushing a tear from her cheek. "But I guess I was wrong."

Kimberly scowled. "He really used the 'it's complicated' line? Next time he comes in, I will personally lace his coffee with Tabasco sauce."

Something between a laugh and a sob burst from

Diana's throat. "Hold that thought. I may still need his help finding homes for these kittens."

"Are you sure? Because if a guy had treated me like that, I'd have trouble being in the same county with him, let alone the same room."

Diana thought back to the trail ride yesterday and Tripp's attempt at an apology. He'd seemed sincere, and really, twelve years had passed. Holding a grudge after all this time certainly didn't speak well of her as a Christian. Besides, if Tripp *had* been the right guy for her, wouldn't God have kept them together somehow? As it was, she'd only hurt herself by letting the fear of having her heart broken again shut down every other relationship she'd had a chance for since then.

Time to put her own words from yesterday into practice and let bygones be bygones. She gathered up her purse and car keys, then hefted the cat box. "The shop's yours for an hour or two, Kim. I'm headed to the animal clinic."

Kimberly followed her to the back door, holding it open as Diana stepped into the alley. "Are you sure you want to do this?"

"Not in the least."

On his lunch break at the clinic, Tripp had just set a bowl of chicken-and-rice soup in the microwave when Yolanda peeked in.

"We have a walk-in," she said. "Stray cat with newborn kittens. Can you take a look?"

"Sure." His next appointment wasn't until three o'clock anyway, so plenty of time to warm up his soup later.

Yolanda pointed him to exam room two and handed

him a folder. "This client's a regular—has several pets of her own. If there's a stray within twenty miles of Juniper Bluff, somehow it finds its way to her."

"A real animal lover, huh?" Tripp could relate.

Then he read the name on the folder tab, and his heart thudded to the pit of his empty stomach. "Diana?"

"Yes, Diana Matthews. Same gal from Diana's Donuts."

"I know." Oh, boy, did he!

The receptionist hesitated, probably confused by the pained look on Tripp's face. "You need me to stay, or can I go to lunch?"

"No, go ahead. I've got it from here." Hauling in a breath, he stepped into the exam room. "Hey, Di...ana."

Her arched brow said she'd caught his near slip of the tongue. "Thanks for working me in. I didn't have anyplace else I could take these kitties."

Kitties. Tripp couldn't help grinning at the tender way she spoke the word. Or the compassionate gleam in her eyes as she stroked the purring mother cat. Laying the folder on the counter, he cast an appraising eye over the scrawny mother cat, a yellow tabby who'd obviously been surviving on her own for a while. The kittens, probably not more than two or three days old, looked healthy enough, but unless their mother got better care so she could feed them, they wouldn't last long.

"Well?" Diana caressed the mother cat's ears. "Can you help me with them?"

"First thing we need to do is get the mother started on some vitamins and quality food." Stethoscope in his ears, Tripp listened to the cat's heart and lungs, then gently palpated her from neck to tail for any signs of growths or infection. The worst he found was matted fur and a small cut on one shoulder, probably from a fight.

The cat wouldn't like what he had to do next, but he needed to take her temperature, check for worms and take a blood sample. Turned out she was a lot more co-operative than Sue Ellen Jamison's Siamese. After setting aside the specimens, Tripp jotted some notes in the file. "The initial results will only take a few minutes. Do you mind waiting?"

"That's fine." Diana's expression remained neutral, but her tone suggested it had taken every ounce of will-power to bring the cats to Tripp.

With a quick smile, he excused himself and slipped down the hall to the lab. When he returned, he found Diana seated on the padded bench with the cat box in her lap.

"You get why I can't keep you," she murmured as she tenderly stroked the mother cat. "I would if I could—" Noticing Tripp, she straightened abruptly and cleared her throat. "What did you find?"

"No visible evidence of worms, and no problems I could see from preliminary tests. I'll have to send samples to our outside lab for a more complete report. That'll take two or three days." Tripp came around the exam table and sat down at the other end of the bench. With the tip of one finger, he rubbed a sleeping kitten's soft, fuzzy belly. "I gather you want help finding homes for these little critters."

Lips in a twist, Diana nodded. "Guess you've seen from my file that I already have a houseful. To borrow a phrase, there's no more room at the inn."

"You always had a soft heart for animals. Remember the baby squirrel—"

"It was so tiny." A tender smile stole across Diana's face. Just as quickly, it vanished. She cleared her throat. "If you can keep the cat and her babies here, I'll put up adoption flyers around town. And I'll cover the vet bill and boarding costs."

"No problem. Since you're a regular, I'm sure we can cut you a deal." Tripp winked. "Or maybe barter vet services for coffee and pastries?"

Diana's eyebrows shot up. "You'd do that?"

"Considering Doc Ingram's affinity for your scones, I think we could twist his arm."

The mother cat was purring loudly now, the sound appearing to have a calming effect on Diana. She glanced up at Tripp. "I appreciate this. More than you know."

Tripp felt like he could sit there all day, basking in the warmth of Diana's presence. Man, how he'd missed this woman! All the years apart seemed to melt away like ice cream on a hot sidewalk, along with all the reasons Tripp had used to justify their breakup.

Maybe…maybe they really could start again. He'd been feeling better every day since getting out of the city. Yes, it had only been a few days now, but his health could only go uphill from here, right? Anyway, in the years since his diagnosis he'd heard of lots of people with Crohn's who went on to live normal, healthy lives, even raised families. Was it possible he'd been too quick to give up on his own chance at happiness?

Diana's sharp sigh brought him back to the present. "I didn't realize how late it was. I need to get back to the shop." She slid the cat box onto the bench between her and Tripp, then stood, her hand lingering on the mother cat's head. With a tentative glance at Tripp, she said, "You'll take good care of them, right?"

"Of course, the very best." He rose as well and picked up the box. "Want to walk back with me and see the kennel where they'll be staying?"

"No, that's okay. I should make this a clean break." She winced, and Tripp could guess exactly where her thoughts had taken her.

"Diana…"

"Gotta run." Her perky smile was back in place. "Tell Doc Ingram y'all can drop in anytime to collect on your coffee and doughnuts. Bye!"

Her brusque departure left him feeling like he'd just been sideswiped by a semi.

And also shocked him back to reality. He had no business entertaining thoughts of rekindling what he and Diana had once shared. She might give lip service to the possibility of starting over as friends, but the flicker of hurt in her eyes made him wonder if she'd ever fully forgive him.

Diana tried hard not to call the clinic every day to check on the mother cat and her babies. Even though Tripp had called a couple of days later to report that mama cat was healthy and her kittens were thriving, Diana couldn't help being concerned. She'd already pre-pared adopt-a-kitten flyers to post around town as soon as the kittens were old enough to leave their mother.

In the meantime, she spent most of her spare time working out details for the therapy pets program. She still needed to enlist her volunteers, but working all day at the doughnut shop didn't leave much time for recruitment efforts. It was the first week of October, and unless Diana had her volunteers lined up and ready by the end of the month, she'd have to postpone Agnes Kraus's evaluation and training visit. Time to speed things up, and tonight's service committee meeting at church might be her best chance.

Around midafternoon, a couple of Main Street business owners stopped in for coffee. Diana cheerfully filled their orders, and the customers had barely sat down at a window table when Tripp and Doc Ingram breezed in.

"Good afternoon, gentlemen. What can I get for you?" Diana tried to keep her attention on Doc Ingram, but her eyes kept betraying her with darting glances at Tripp. The last time she'd actually seen him was at church last Sunday, and then only in passing. Seth and Christina had kept him occupied as they introduced him to the pastor and other acquaintances.

"Two coffees, for starters." Doc palmed his Stetson. "Then I'd like to bend your ear about catering an open house for us at the clinic."

"Sure. Meet me at the corner table over there and you can tell me all about it." Diana filled two mugs, then a third one for herself. As she set the mugs on a tray, she remembered Tripp had asked for soy milk on his first visit, so she filled a small ceramic pitcher. Still wearing her pink Diana's Donuts apron over her T-shirt and jeans, she carried the tray to the table.

As she distributed the mugs and handed Tripp the container of soy milk, his smile conveyed both appreciation and surprise. "Thanks," he murmured in the mellow tone that once set her heart racing.

And apparently still did, if the heat rising up her cheeks meant anything.

She straightened her apron and took the chair on the other side of Doc Ingram. "So. About your open house. When is it, and what's the occasion?"

"If it's not too short notice, I'm thinking next Sunday afternoon, say from two to four," the doc answered. "It'll be a welcome party for Tripp here, a chance for the community to drop in and meet him."

"Sounds fun." With a smile and nod in Tripp's direction, Diana pulled a pen and notepad from her apron pocket and jotted down the date. "What would you like to serve?"

"Thought I'd leave the menu in your capable hands." Doc chuckled. "Consider it part of Tripp's bartering agreement for seeing to those cats you dropped off last week."

Tripp caught Diana's eye and mouthed, *Not my idea.*

Something she should have guessed. Tripp had never been much of a socializer. If they went out with friends, there would be only one or two other couples. If someone hosted a party, Tripp would steer Diana to the less noisy perimeter, and he was always ready to say their goodbyes long before Diana had run out of conversation.

She gave a mental shrug. One more indication they weren't right for each other.

"I was teasing about the cat thing," Doc Ingram said. "Planned on doing this anyway, so I'm more than glad to pay."

"No, it's perfectly all right. A deal's a deal." Diana tapped the pen against her lips as she considered what to serve. "We can do coffee, doughnuts, minimuffins… and maybe some cranberry punch for the kids."

"Great. I'll start getting the word out." As Doc Ingram took a sip of his coffee, his cell phone chirped. Reading a text, he grimaced. "Horse down with colic at the Hendersons'. Gotta skedaddle. Hate to strand you, Tripp, but the Henderson ranch is clear the opposite direction from the clinic."

"No problem," Tripp said. "I'll find my own way back."

Halfway to the door, the doc halted and snapped his fingers, a mischievous look curling his lips. "Hey, since your appointment calendar's clear for the rest of the day, why don't you hang out here? Y'all can hash out the open house menu together."

Suddenly nervous, Diana arched a brow. But with only a few customers and Kimberly covering the counter, she didn't have an obvious reason to excuse herself. She offered Tripp an empathetic smile. "So… an open house, huh?"

He hiked one shoulder. "Like I said, not my idea."

"It's a small-town thing. People like to get to know the folks they're doing business with."

"That's one part of this job I already appreciate. People are way more relaxed and friendly than at the Austin clinic I came from."

Something in Tripp's tone evoked a pang of concern. "I thought opening your own big-city vet practice had always been your goal."

"I thought so, too…at first." His jaw edged sideways. He sat forward as if on the verge of saying more, but then he abruptly stood and picked up his mug. "Think I could trade this for a glass of water?"

"Keep your seat. I'll get it." Diana bustled over to the counter and signaled Kimberly.

Handing Diana a glass of ice water, Kimberly wiggled her brows. "Looks like y'all are having a real nice chat over there. Mending some fences?"

Diana hesitated, wondering the same thing herself. Her tone became wistful as she murmured, "Maybe we are."

Tripp tried not to stare as Diana sauntered back to the table with his water. Since his first glimpse two Saturdays ago, he couldn't get enough of looking at her. The way she walked. The way her long, tapered fingers held her horse's reins or caressed those tiny kittens. The way she flicked a loose strand of hair out of her eyes or tossed her perky ponytail.

She set the glass in front of him, then shifted from foot to foot. "Unless you have more thoughts about Sunday's menu, I should probably get back to work."

"Right." Biting back a smile, Tripp nodded toward the only other two customers in the shop. "I can see you're super busy right now."

She rolled her eyes, another endearing gesture he recalled all too well from when they were dating. "Well… I do have a few things to catch up on in the office. I *am* the owner, after all."

"Of course, sorry. I'll just finish up here and be on my way."

Nodding, Diana started to turn away, then swiveled to face him again. "But how will you get back to the clinic?"

Tripp shrugged. "It's only a mile or two. I can hoof it."

Just then, Diana's blond assistant bustled over. She carried a square white box with a cellophane lid. "Diana, can you run these pastries over to Alan's insurance office? They're for his staff meeting in the morning."

Suspicion clouded Diana's expression. "But Alan usually comes by early on Wednesday mornings to pick up his order."

"I know, but he's always so rushed, and I've got this batch fresh out of the oven, so I thought, why not save him the trip?"

Smiling to himself, Tripp watched the play of emotions across Diana's face—confusion, consternation, then the clear realization that Kimberly was playing her. Arms crossed, Diana glared at her assistant. "And is there some pressing reason *you* can't drop them off?"

"I have more muffins in the oven." Kimberly held the box out to Diana. "You can take Alan his pastries, then give Doc Willoughby a ride to the clinic."

Talk about obvious! Tripp took another swallow of water and pushed back his chair. "I told you, Diana, I can walk. Don't put yourself out on my account."

"Oh, she wouldn't be," Kimberly gushed. "This is perfect, Diana. While you're there, you can visit your kitties." Winking, she added, "You *know* you want to."

Diana chewed her lip. "Well, I *would* like to see how they're doing." Relaxing her stance, she took the box from Kimberly, then glanced uncertainly at Tripp. "You wouldn't mind?"

He wasn't particularly happy about being set up, but spending more time with Diana? That he didn't mind in the least. "You're welcome to visit anytime."

Ten minutes later, he waited in Diana's SUV outside the Alan Glazer Insurance Agency while Diana delivered the pastries.

Returning to the car, she frowned as she climbed in behind the wheel. "That was awkward."

"Problems?" Tripp asked.

"I had to reassure Alan we weren't trying to pawn off last weekend's stale leftovers." Mouth in a twist, she looked like she blamed Tripp for the awkwardness.

Didn't she get this was all Kimberly's doing? Tripp was just an innocent bystander.

Okay, not exactly innocent. Apparently, there was no statute of limitations for breaking someone's heart. Tripp doubted Diana would have yielded to Kimberly's ploy if not for the chance of visiting the kittens.

So he'd take what he could get. In the meantime, he'd keep chipping away at the gigantic wall Diana had erected around her heart.

They arrived at the clinic a few minutes later. As Tripp led the way through the rear entrance, the three dogs they were boarding for vacationers started yipping.

"It's just me, fellas." Tripp opened the door to the dog kennel wing, and the noise grew louder. "Calm down, okay? Suppertime isn't for another couple of hours."

Hands over her ears, Diana grimaced. "This is why I have cats."

"Wimp." Tripp grinned and shut the door. "I think you'll find the feline quarters a bit quieter."

He showed Diana along a short corridor and into a room with two tiers of spacious cat kennels along one wall. Most of the kennels were vacant, except for the upper kennel on the near end with the mother cat and kittens, and at the other, a cat recuperating from minor surgery. Opposite the kennels stood a large tank with colorful tropical fish lazily swimming about.

Eyes widening, Diana glanced around briefly, then

strode over to peek at the kittens, snuggled up to their mother on a snowy fleece pad. "Wow, I had no idea how plush your kennels were."

Tripp had been quite impressed as well when Doc Ingram gave him the tour. "You've never been back here before?"

"No, my parents or a neighbor always take care of my pets when I'm away." She poked her fingers through the grate to scratch the mother cat behind the ears.

"You can open the door," Tripp said, stepping closer. "Here, let me." He reached for the latch at the same moment she did. When his hand closed over hers, she flinched. He knew he should back off, but he let his hand linger.

Diana's breath quickened. "Tripp…"

"Sorry." Throat raspy, he dropped his hand to his side and edged away, giving Diana space to open the kennel door. When she leaned in to love on the cat and kittens, the mother cat's purring could be heard clear across the room.

Maybe the sound would drown out the pounding of Tripp's pulse. Yep, he was just plain crazy for thinking he could keep things platonic, when everything in him wanted to fight to win Diana back. But until he felt ready to confide in her about the real reason they'd broken up, he didn't dare try.

"They're growing so fast." Diana turned from the kennel, a serene smile replacing the tension of moments ago. "The kittens' eyes should open soon, and then they'll start getting playful."

Glad for the distraction from his going-nowhere train of thought, Tripp grinned. "Kittens are fun. It's cute when they act like miniature wild beasts on the hunt."

"Still wish I could keep them, or at least one of the kittens." Latching the kennel, Diana stiffened her shoulders. "But, alas, I must be strong and resist temptation."

Tripp released a nervous chuckle as he opened the door to the corridor. "Thanks again for the lift. I'm sure you've got a million other things to do."

"It was worth the extra trouble to spend some time with the kitties." Diana paused in the doorway, her cheeks reddening. "I didn't mean that the way it sounded."

A barely suppressed sigh caught in Tripp's throat. "It's okay. I totally get it."

"Do you?" Diana gave her head a quick shake. "Because I'm not sure I do." Stepping into the hallway, she swiveled to face the wall, her gaze fixed on a poster depicting the life cycle of fleas. "I'm trying, Tripp. Really trying to deal with having you back in my life. I'm working on letting go of the past, but this—this *friendship* thing isn't always as easy as I'd like it to be."

Tripp swallowed over the thickness in his throat. "Believe me, Diana, if I could go back and change the way I handled things, I would. Breaking up with you was the last thing I wanted to do."

She tossed a pain-filled glance over her shoulder. "Obviously not, since your career apparently became a much higher priority."

"That isn't how it was. I mean, yes, my vet studies were pretty demanding back then, but—" Palming his forehead, Tripp silenced himself before he revealed more than he was ready to. Besides, his belly had just issued an unpleasant warning. He inhaled and tried again. "I messed up, okay? And I realize no amount of apologizing is going to make up for it. But I still care about you, Di. I never stopped caring."

Her chin quivered. At least she hadn't smacked him for calling her Di. "God's been working with me on this forgiveness thing for quite a while now, and I'm making progress, I promise." Turning toward the exit, she blew out a distracted breath. "But now, I really do have to go."

Tripp followed her out to her car. Grasping for even one more minute with her, he blurted, "How's it going with the therapy pets thing?"

"Slow but sure. I'm hoping to get some support from our church's service committee tonight." Diana fished in her purse for her car keys.

"I started to tell you the other day, I worked with a therapy pets group during my veterinary internship. If there's anything I can do to help—" The moment the words left his mouth, he could tell he'd overstepped.

"Thanks, but I've got everything under control." With a brisk nod, Diana climbed into her car.

Watching her drive away, Tripp wondered if there'd ever come a time when she wouldn't look at him through eyes clouded by the past.

Leaving the clinic, Diana suffered a twinge of guilt at how abruptly she'd rejected Tripp's offer of help. It was just way too soon to involve him in her life any more than necessary. Besides, the therapy pets project was her idea. She didn't need Tripp, or anyone else, waltzing in and taking over.

After wrapping up end-of-the-day office work at the doughnut shop, she hurried home to feed her menagerie and warm up a microwave dinner for herself, then drove over to the church. Pastor Terry had just opened the meeting as Diana slid into one of the last empty chairs at the conference table. She scribbled a few notes while the other members reported on completed and current service projects, but mostly her mind raced with thoughts of how to persuade the committee to consider adopting her therapy pets venture as a church outreach.

When her turn finally came, she opened her file folder of notes and cleared her throat. "I know this is a little different from the service projects we've done in the past, but I believe it could bless not only the recipients but anyone who volunteers, as well."

She went on to talk about her great-aunt's move to the assisted-living center and how hard it was for Aunt Jennie to part with her precious corgi. "That's what gave me the idea, so I've done a lot of research and have contacted a therapy pets organization about starting a group right here in Juniper Bluff."

As she described the requirements and training process, a few heads began to nod around the table, while other committee members looked skeptical.

"It sounds good in principle," a woman across the table said. "But if having a friendly, well-behaved dog isn't good enough...sorry, but I don't have the time or the money to invest in obedience training."

Others voiced similar thoughts. Only two people expressed interest, saying their dogs had completed basic obedience classes and asking Diana to keep them posted as plans progressed. When Pastor Terry asked for a motion to table the discussion until their November meeting, Diana's heart sank. As slow as this committee operated, even if they did decide to get behind the plan as one of their service projects, it would likely be the first of the year or later before Diana could expect to see any action.

Anyway, by the end of the meeting, the committee had jumped on someone's suggestion to put Christmas care packages together for the Camp Serenity kids. Diana reluctantly agreed the idea made more sense for the committee as a whole, but she couldn't help feeling discouraged.

After the meeting adjourned, Pastor Terry stopped Diana on her way to her car. "Sorry about the lack of support for your therapy pets project. Have you thought about putting up some flyers at the vet clinic? I'm sure Doc Ingram and his new partner would be happy to help spread the word."

Diana had to admit the pastor was right. What better place to connect with pet owners than a veterinary clinic? "Thanks, I'll think about it."

"You might consider *praying* about it," Pastor Terry said with a knowing smile. At her questioning look, he continued, "I heard through the grapevine that there might be a bit of history between you and Juniper Bluff's newest resident. Anytime you'd like to talk…"

Heaving a sigh, Diana leaned against her car door. "It's true, Tripp and I dated in college, and it didn't end well. The day he walked into my doughnut shop and I found out he'd moved to Juniper Bluff, I felt blindsided."

"Because you still have feelings for him." It was a statement, not a question.

"No. Yes. I don't know!" A growl rumbling in her throat, Diana tipped her head to gaze into the starry sky. "It's been twelve years. I should have been over him a long time ago."

"But since you aren't…" Pastor Terry lifted one

shoulder. "Maybe your heart is trying to tell you something."

It was a thought Diana couldn't quite bring herself to entertain. She turned slowly and pulled open her car door. "I just don't want to make the same mistake twice."

The pastor chuckled. "Then I repeat my earlier advice. *Pray.*"

Giving a meek nod, Diana climbed into her car. "I will, Pastor. Thanks."

Chapter Four

It was Sunday before Tripp saw Diana again, which was about five days longer than he'd have liked. But he couldn't bring himself to pop in at the doughnut shop and disconcert her any more than he already had.

As he joined Robert Ingram and his family in church that morning, he glimpsed Diana across the sanctuary. He looked forward to even a brief moment to say hello after the service, but by the time he made it out to the foyer, she'd disappeared.

"You'll see her this afternoon at the open house," Robert said as if reading Tripp's thoughts.

Tripp shrugged. "If she hasn't already delegated the catering job to her assistant."

"Diana has too much pride in her business reputation. Don't worry. She'll be there." With an elbow to Tripp's ribs, Robert motioned toward the double doors. "Better get a move on. Emily'll have a conniption if we let Sunday dinner get cold."

Tripp had to admit, everyone in Juniper Bluff—with one notable exception—had made him feel warmly welcomed. The Austins and Petersons out at Serenity Hills had extended several invitations to join them for supper at the main house, and Tripp had quickly learned he'd be a fool to turn down one of Marie Peterson's home-cooked meals. Today would be his second time to have Sunday dinner with the Ingrams, and if last week's pot roast was any indication, Emily's cooking could compete with Marie's any day.

One problem, though—if he wanted to continue accepting these invitations, he'd eventually have to say something about the Crohn's. He'd already earned a few concerned glances from his hostesses after discreetly leaving some of the more troublesome foods untouched.

It happened again at lunch when Emily Ingram tried to load his plate with her crispy fried chicken and a green salad teeming with raw veggies. Just thinking about what those foods could do to his system gave him a belly cramp.

Emily frowned as she returned a huge chicken thigh to the platter. "Surely you can eat more than one teensy piece of white meat. You're not much more than skin and bones, young man."

True, he'd dropped several pounds in the years since his diagnosis, but he was eating healthier than ever. He'd learned which foods caused him problems, though, and if he wanted to avoid a flare-up, he had to be picky. "It all looks delicious, but I'm saving plenty of room for your baked squash casserole. Robert told me it's his favorite."

The compliment seemed to mollify her, even more so when Tripp asked for a second and then a third helping of the tasty dish. He'd learned long ago that steamed or baked veggies were his friends, so he figured he'd better eat as much as he could so he wouldn't be tempted by Diana's pastries at the open house.

After helping with the kitchen cleanup, Tripp left for the clinic with Robert so they could open up for Diana. A few minutes later, she arrived with Kimberly and a teenage boy Tripp remembered seeing at the doughnut shop. Tripp stayed out of the way as they arranged baked goods, coffee urns and a cold beverage dispenser on cloth-covered tables set up in the reception area. As Tripp watched them work with practiced efficiency, his admiration for Diana grew even stronger. She really had done well for herself here in Juniper Bluff—and was probably a lot happier living among her hometown family and friends than she would have been if things had worked out between them. Even without his health issues, Tripp's long hours completing his veterinary degree, followed by an even heavier schedule working at a big-city vet clinic, meant they'd have enjoyed precious little time together as newlyweds.

Newlyweds. Exactly what he'd expected them to be twelve years ago.

Until the Crohn's.

Sometimes he got downright angry with God for allowing this disease into his life. Even angrier that it had compelled him to give up the woman he loved. He'd tried hard to learn from the example of Saint Paul, to be content with his circumstances and accept whatever God wanted him to learn from his own "thorn in the flesh."

Then again, God had brought him to Juniper Bluff— surely not to torture him with an almost daily reminder of what might have been. Even if the only reason was so that Tripp could set things right with Diana, he'd do his best and be grateful for the opportunity.

Watching Diana at work, he hadn't noticed how deeply he'd sank into his musings until Robert came over and stood right in front of him. "Excuse me, Doc Willoughby, but this is *your* day. Time to smile and mingle."

"Sorry, got distracted."

"Obviously." With a wry grin, Robert steered Tripp over to a cluster of middle-aged women chatting near the coffee urn.

One of them was Sue Ellen Jamison, whose cat Cleopatra had done a number on Tripp's hand his first day at the clinic. "Look, girls, here's Doc Willoughby now," Sue Ellen chirped. "My Cleo's new favorite vet, and mine, too!"

"Now, Sue Ellen," Robert said, "you're gonna hurt my feelings if you keep talking like that."

Tripp offered polite greetings to Sue Ellen and her friends and tried to ignore their flirtatious winks. They were all old enough to be his mother anyway, which reminded him he needed to give Brooke a call later and find out how Mom was doing.

Stifling a pang of worry, he let his gaze stray to where Diana served punch and pastries to a few of the children who'd arrived with their parents.

She glanced up briefly. When their eyes met, her hand faltered and she overfilled a punch cup. With a startled gasp, she grabbed some napkins to mop up the spill.

Robert's firm grip bit into Tripp's shoulder. "Why don't you get it over with and go talk to her?"

Tripp shot his partner a mock glare. "With friends like you—"

"—the world would be a happier place. Just do it already." Grinning mischievously, Robert gave Tripp a not-so-gentle shove.

He barely kept himself from tripping. Diana's smirk said she'd noticed. By the time he made his way across the crowded reception area, she'd poured him a cup of punch. Their fingertips grazed as she handed it to him.

He sipped gratefully, the tangy cranberry concoction soothing his dry throat. "This is really good. Thanks."

Her gaze slid to just below the level of his chin, and she hiked a brow. "Wow, a tie and everything. Dressing to impress?"

"Just trying to look professional." Tripp had debated about wearing a sports coat and was glad he'd decided not to. The ladies wore their Sunday best, but jeans, boots and open-neck shirts seemed to be the wardrobe of choice for the younger males of the community, no matter what day of the week.

"Well, you look very nice." Diana offered him a plate and napkin. "Care for a pastry? You're the guest of honor, after all."

"Don't remind me." Knowing he shouldn't—and wouldn't—eat it, out of politeness Tripp chose a blueberry minimuffin and set it on his plate. He smiled and nodded as Sue Ellen and her friends crossed in front of him for coffee refills.

"Just breathe," Diana murmured as she filled punch cups for two youngsters. "Only one hour and forty-three minutes to go."

"You're all heart." It was encouraging to think Diana felt comfortable enough to joke with him, but Tripp suspected the jibes were only her self-defense mechanism kicking in.

For the next hour and a half, the continual ebb and flow of guests diverted Tripp's attention, a good thing since the ground beneath his feet never felt totally stable with Diana nearby.

By the time four o'clock rolled around, most of the guests had said their goodbyes. Tripp shook hands with the last family to depart and said he looked forward to meeting their pets very soon. Even though he'd relaxed a bit as the warm welcomes flowed over him, he whistled a sigh of relief that the open house was finally over.

Turning from the door, he saw Diana and her helpers starting to pack up the leftover pastries. Diana pointed to the plate he'd set down earlier with his uneaten minimuffin. "Want this now, or should I add it to the other goodies I'm boxing up for you?"

A boxful of sugar-laden doughnuts and muffins was the last thing Tripp needed, but he figured Seth Austin's kids would appreciate the treats. He ambled over to the table. "Guess I got too busy visiting to eat."

"It was a nice turnout. You'll be the talk of the town for weeks." Diana closed the lid on the box, then began gathering up the remaining plates and napkins.

"Anything I can do to help?"

Diana cast him a dismissive glance and kept working. "No, thanks. We've got it handled."

He couldn't help feeling stung by her refusal. With a tight smile, he backed away.

He hadn't taken two steps when his cell phone vibrated in his pants pocket. Reading his sister's name on the display, he pressed the answer icon. "Hey, Brooke, I was going to call you later."

"Tripp, I've got bad news. Mom's been admitted to the hospital."

Moments after Tripp answered his cell phone, the sudden change in his expression made Diana's heart clench. Twisting sideways, shoulders hunched, he looked as if he'd been caught off guard by disturbing news.

Kimberly returned from emptying the coffee urn. She paused next to Diana. "Is Tripp okay?"

"Not sure." Diana gnawed on her lower lip. This appeared to be much more serious than someone's pet needing emergency treatment.

"Maybe you should find out. He looks pretty upset."

Diana wasn't so sure Tripp would welcome her intrusion. Glancing around, she hoped to enlist Doc Ingram's help but then remembered seeing him escort a couple of older ladies out to their car.

Tripp spoke a few more words into his phone, then disconnected. Still facing away, he heaved a shaky breath.

Diana couldn't restrain herself a moment longer. She scurried around the serving table, stopping just short of laying a hand on Tripp's arm. "Is—is there anything I can do?"

He seemed surprised to see her standing there. His Adam's apple bobbed with a pained swallow. "That was Brooke. My mom's in the hospital."

"Oh, no! What happened?" Diana had sweet memories of Peggy Willoughby, the soft-spoken woman who had welcomed her into their family like a daughter.

"Mom has kidney disease. It was causing some heart problems, so they hospitalized her to get things under control."

"Kidney disease? Tripp, I had no idea."

"It's been going on for a while. That's why Brooke got my folks to move out to California, so she could help with Mom's care."

Diana hadn't even known Brooke was living in California now. After college, they'd lost touch. At a loss for words, she motioned toward a row of chairs. "Sit down. Let me get you some water or something."

"No, thanks." Groaning, he pressed a hand to his side. "I think I just need to get out of here."

"Tripp—"

Before Diana could say more, he pushed through the inner door and marched down the hallway. His thudding footsteps faded, and moments later, the rear door slammed.

Kimberly, who'd continued quietly packing up their catering supplies, sidled over. "I couldn't help overhearing. Sounds like his mom's pretty sick."

"I feel horrible for him. For his whole family."

"Guess you got pretty close to them, before…"

Diana nodded. "I loved them all, very much. After we broke up, it felt like I'd lost them, too."

Doc Ingram returned through the front entrance, his expression grim. "Caught Tripp as he was leaving. Said he wasn't feeling well and to apologize for taking off so quickly without thanking you again."

"Our pleasure," Kimberly answered when Diana couldn't seem to find her voice. "We'll just finish up here and be on our way."

Brushing aside her troubled thoughts, Diana joined

Kimberly and Ethan in loading their catering supplies onto a rolling cart. Twenty minutes later, Diana parked in the alley behind the doughnut shop, and shortly after they'd carried everything inside.

"Ethan and I can put all this stuff away," Kimberly offered. "Go home. You look beat."

Diana couldn't deny she was exhausted, both physically and emotionally. Maintaining her composure around Tripp made everything harder, and the heart-breaking news about his mother only added to her distress.

She gave Kimberly a grateful hug. "Offer accepted. I'll come in extra early in the morning to help you with the doughnuts."

Back in her car, Diana started for home. Before she'd driven two blocks, she had a flashback to the pained look on Tripp's face in the moments before he'd left the clinic. He'd never been the type to burden others with his personal problems, and now she pictured him alone in his cabin, racked with worry while he waited for more news from his sister.

At the next intersection, with no traffic in either direction, Diana braked and rested her head on the steering wheel. Her conscience was telling her to go to him, but her heart resisted. *What should I do, God?*

Her conscience spoke a little louder, which she took as God's direction to put her misgivings aside and do the right thing. If she were a stranger in a new community, she'd certainly be grateful for the support of an old friend at a time like this.

Old friend. After what they'd meant to each other—what she'd *believed* they'd meant to each other—could she really bear to settle for friendship?

Did she have a choice?

With a resigned sigh, Diana flipped on her turn signal. Two right turns took her back toward town. She passed the square, then turned left onto the farm road leading to Serenity Hills. She couldn't be sure he'd gone straight to his cabin, but if he hadn't, she'd wait for him.

Arriving at the guest ranch, she followed the lane around to the staff cabins. When she spotted Tripp's dark green SUV, she suffered a moment of panic—could she really do this?

Before she could change her mind, Tripp stepped onto the porch. He still wore his dress shirt, the sleeves rolled up to his elbows and his tie hanging loose from his open collar.

As she pulled up beside his car, his eyes widened in surprise. He came down the steps to meet her. "Diana, what are you doing here?"

Nudging the door closed with her hip, she crossed her arms and forced herself to meet his gaze. "I couldn't stop worrying about…your mom."

"She'd appreciate knowing that." Tripp ducked his head. "I do, too."

Diana narrowed her gaze. "You didn't tell Doc Ingram about your mom, did you?"

Guilt furrowing his brow, Tripp glanced away with a shrug. "I will, when I know more."

"This is so like you, Tripp, always holding things in." Sarcasm riddled her tone. "So what are you planning to do in the meantime? Pull your 'Mr. Cool' routine and go on about your business like nothing's wrong?"

"If you drove all the way out here to lecture me—"

"I drove all the way out here because I thought you could use a friend."

Jaw muscles bunched, he stared at her for a full second. "Yeah," he said, his voice husky. "Guess maybe I could." He plowed stiff fingers through his hair. "Sorry, it's been kind of a roller-coaster day."

"For both of us." This time she didn't hold back from touching his arm. "Your mom will always be special to me. I hope you know that."

"I do. I wish—" Tripp squeezed his eyes shut, then shook his head as if trying to clear it. "Never mind. Just…thanks for coming. It means a lot."

Diana wondered what he'd been about to say but decided she might be better off not knowing. She nodded toward the two red chairs on the porch. "Since I'm here, maybe we could sit for a while and work on this friendship thing?"

Tripp answered with a soft chuckle. "I'd like that."

Sitting on the porch with Diana was nice…real nice. Tripp had never in a million years anticipated her showing up like this, offering friendship and, at least figuratively, a shoulder to lean on while he waited for word about his mother.

Diana gazed toward a nearby pasture where two mares grazed. "Did Brooke say when to expect more news?"

"She promised to call back after they get Mom stabilized." Tripp spoke with more confidence than he felt. Each setback seemed worse than the one before, and he worried how much longer he'd have his mom around.

"I hate that she's going through this." Diana's fists knotted on the armrests. "Isn't there anything they can do? Maybe a kidney transplant or something?"

"It's not that simple. Blood type, tissue matching—a

lot of things have to come together for a kidney dona-tion to be successful."

"And no one in your family was a match?"

"We all got tested, but…it didn't work out." The fa-miliar lump of regret landed hard in the pit of Tripp's belly. He stood and paced to the porch rail. Glancing back at Diana, he pasted on a smile. "Mind if we talk about something else? Tell me how your therapy pets project is going."

Her shoulders sagged. "Things aren't moving as quickly as I'd hoped." She told him about the cool recep-tion from the church committee members, then added hesitantly, "I was planning to ask you today if I could post flyers at the clinic, until…"

Sidestepping the subject of his mother's illness, Tripp said, "Sure, of course you can. I told you I'd help any way I could." He returned to his chair. Forearms braced on his knees, he continued thoughtfully, "Obedience certification is usually the biggest hurdle. Once we get some interested dog owners, we can find a trainer and schedule the classes. Then it's just a matter of—"

"Tripp."

He met her tight-lipped stare.

"I only asked you about posting flyers, not to take charge of *my* project."

Straightening, he cleared his throat. "Didn't mean to. Guess I got a little carried away."

Diana faced forward. "I'm a little touchy, I suppose."

She didn't have to spell it out. He lifted his hands in a gesture of surrender. "Really sorry, okay? This is me backing off."

"And now you're just mocking me." Her voice trembled the tiniest bit, the pitiful sound tying knots around Tripp's heart.

"I'd never mock you, Diana. I care—" He cut himself off before he said too much.

For a microsecond he thought he glimpsed a spark of hope in her eyes, before she covered it with an indifferent shrug. "This is silly. You said you've had experience working with therapy pets, and since I have no idea what I'm doing, I'd be a fool to refuse your help."

He wanted so badly to take her hand, to tell her how incredibly cute she looked with that conciliatory pout on her lips. His voice fell to just above a whisper. "Whatever you need, just ask."

With a sharp exhale, she muttered, "Thank you."

Several minutes of silence passed while the warm afternoon breeze swept away the remnants of their quarrel. Tripp chose to concentrate on the fact that Diana was here and speaking to him at all, which meant there had to be some hope for them, right? How many times had he prayed for this chance to clear the air between them, to somehow make up for the hurt he'd caused?

Tell her.

His inner voice just wouldn't shut up. But he couldn't tell her, not yet. Not until their connection as friends in the present overshadowed the heartbreak of the past.

"You're right," Diana said, interrupting his thoughts.

He shot her a startled glance. "I am? About what?"

"Obedience classes. How soon do you think we could set something up?"

Smiling to himself, Tripp tried to keep any hint of smugness out of his tone. Her use of the word *we* wasn't lost on him. "I'll make some calls first thing in the morning."

"Great. I'll get on my computer and work on those flyers tonight. As soon as business slows down at the shop tomorrow, I'll bring them by."

"Or…maybe we could meet somewhere for lunch?" Tripp figured he was expecting too much, but he couldn't stop himself from asking. "By then, I might have some answers for you about a dog trainer."

Diana appeared to be thinking over his suggestion. At least she hadn't given him an outright no. "The supermarket deli has an outdoor café. Would twelve thirty work for you?"

Tripp couldn't believe she'd agreed. "Sounds good."

Checking her watch, Diana sighed. "I should go. My *kids* will be wanting their supper." She pushed up from the chair. "When you hear from Brooke again, would you give me a call?"

"Of course."

"Promise me? I don't care if it's the middle of the night. I'd like to know."

Tripp crossed his heart. "I promise." He followed her down the porch steps. "Diana?"

She turned. "Yes?"

"Thanks."

Her brusque nod told him he didn't have to explain. "See you tomorrow."

Seconds later, she drove away, leaving Tripp with a bittersweet ache in his chest.

Too anxious about his mother to think about supper, Tripp made do with scrambled eggs and a slice of Canadian bacon. For the next hour or two, he tried to distract himself by reading up on the latest heartworm preventatives. When Brooke hadn't called by 10 p.m., his frustration got the best of him. He grabbed his cell phone off the lamp table and rang Brooke's number.

"Tripp, sorry for not calling sooner." She sounded tired.

"I've been going crazy. How's Mom?"

"Hold on a sec. I'm stepping into the corridor." The ambient sounds coming through the phone grew louder—indistinct voices, random beeps, the rattle of wheels across tile. "Okay, I can talk now. They got Mom's blood pressure stabilized about an hour ago."

"Thank God!" Tripp ran his hand across his eyes.

"We're not out of the woods yet. This was pretty serious." Brooke's voice faltered. "Tripp, the doctor said we need to be prepared."

A knot lodged in Tripp's throat. "Prepared?"

"Mom's weakening. Even if they found a kidney donor tomorrow, it wouldn't help. Her health has deteriorated too much."

For the millionth time, Tripp blamed the Crohn's that made him ineligible to give his mother a kidney. Barely able to speak the words, he asked, "How long?"

"The doctor won't commit to a timetable. He says it all depends on how well she rallies after this setback."

Tripp stood and paced the small sitting area. "Should I fly out there? I can leave in the morning—"

"No, Tripp." Brooke released a long sigh. "If you come now, it would only reinforce to both Mom and Dad that we're expecting the worst. I want to keep their hopes up for as long as we can."

Her logic made sense, but Tripp hated having his family so far away at a time like this. "All right, but if you even suspect—" He had to swallow hard before

"Among other things," Kimberly muttered with a smirk.

Diana shot her assistant a get-lost glare.

"Try lavender essential oil on your pillow," Kelly suggested. "A couple of drops work wonders when you can't relax."

"Thanks, I'll remember that." Diana tucked Kelly's receipt and some napkins onto the tray.

"And keep me posted about your group. I've got a sweet rescue dog I think would make a great therapy pet."

Diana perked up. While waiting to hear from Tripp last night, she'd finished designing and printing out copies of her informational flyer. She'd placed a few on the counter and handed one to Kelly. "I'm working with Visiting Pet Pals. This explains some of their requirements. My cell number's at the bottom, so give me a call if you'd like to get involved."

"I will." Giving a nod, Kelly added the flyer to her coffee tray, then hurried out.

With another glance at the time, Diana stifled a groan. Still an hour and twenty minutes before she was supposed to meet Tripp for lunch. As distraught as he'd been yesterday, would he even remember their plans, much less that he'd promised to make inquiries about dog trainers? She considered calling him at the clinic with a friendly reminder but quickly trashed the thought. As much as the therapy pets project meant to her, it was nothing compared to what Tripp's family was going through.

Business slowed again as folks returned to their offices and shops. While Diana tidied the coffee service area, Kimberly consolidated the remaining doughnuts and pastries at the front of the display case.

Finishing, Kimberly peeled off her food prep gloves and dropped them in the trash. She gave Diana's shoulder a friendly poke. "Take off, why don't you? I can tell you're chomping at the bit to get out of here."

Diana grimaced. It was past eleven thirty now. She could brood just as easily sitting outside the supermarket deli as she could finding busywork at the doughnut shop—*and* she wouldn't have to fend off Kimberly's prying questions. She slipped out of her apron. "Thanks, I do have some…errands to run."

Kimberly winked. "If you happen to run into Doc Willoughby, give him my regards."

With a disbelieving glance toward the ceiling, Diana hung up her apron and marched to the office to grab her purse.

By noon she'd ordered an iced green tea and carried it to one of the umbrella-shaded tables outside the deli. From there, she had a good view of both the parking lot and the supermarket entrance. She also laid her cell phone on the table in case Tripp called or texted.

Then, annoyed with herself, she jammed the phone back into her purse and shifted her chair sideways. What had gotten into her, letting herself get so keyed up about seeing Tripp again? There was nothing between them, and this wasn't a date. Why should she—

Her cell phone chimed. She dove for her purse. Reading Tripp's name on the phone's display screen, she took a deep breath before answering. "Hi. Are you on your way?"

"I'm stuck at the clinic," Tripp said. "Last-minute appointment. Afraid I can't make it for lunch, after all."

"Oh." Diana clamped her teeth together to stifle an unexpected wave of disappointment. "Okay, then. Guess we'll talk later."

"Sure. But I wanted to tell you I did get hold of a dog trainer this morning."

"That's great. Thank you." Gazing across the parking lot, Diana sighed. "I…I figured the therapy pets thing might be the furthest thing from your mind this morning."

Tripp uttered a weak chuckle. "Actually, it's helping to keep my mind off other things—which I really need right now."

"Then I'm glad to be of assistance." Diana reached into her purse for a pen and a scrap of paper. "If you have the dog trainer's number…"

"Actually, I wondered if you'd be free later this afternoon. I thought we could drive over to the pet shop where he works in Fredericksburg and meet with him in person."

"You really don't have to do that, Tripp. I can take it from here."

"You'd be doing me a favor if you let me tag along." His tone softened. "Like I said, I need the distraction."

How could she refuse? After a quick review of her schedule, Diana agreed, and Tripp offered to pick her up at the doughnut shop around three thirty. They said goodbye, and Diana returned to the deli to pick up a salad to go—although the thought of lunching alone at her desk evoked an empty feeling in the pit of her stomach that was far more disconcerting than hunger pangs.

About time you admitted it, she told herself. *You were actually looking forward to having lunch with Tripp.*

Well, she'd have her chance to spend time with him

later when they drove to Fredericksburg. Except she'd better keep her priorities straight and remember this outing was strictly business.

Back at work, though, she found herself doing too much clock watching. At three twenty, she turned the shop over to Kimberly and stepped out the front door to wait for Tripp.

He'd just driven up. Climbing into the passenger seat of his SUV, she said, "You're early."

"So are you," he answered with a grin. "Ready to head over to the pet shop?"

"Let's go." Diana buckled her seat belt and slid on the cheap new pair of sunglasses she'd bought after the horseback riding fiasco. "By the way, I brought some flyers for you to take back to the clinic—that is, if it's still okay."

"Absolutely."

Tripp fell silent as he headed toward the highway, and Diana was having trouble coming up with scintillating travel conversation.

Then Tripp broke the silence with a long sigh. "I just wanted to say... I mean, if I got a little emotional last night..."

Diana glanced over, noting the embarrassed twist to his lips. "You had every right," she said. "I can't even imagine how worried you must be."

"Still, I shouldn't have burdened you with my problems."

Annoyance tightened Diana's chest. This was Tripp being Tripp, so why should she be surprised? "It's no burden. That's what friends are for."

He met her gaze with an uncertain smile before returning his attention to the road. "You're right. Thanks."

A few minutes later, they arrived at the pet store. Tripp asked one of the clerks to page Sean, and shortly a shaggy-haired young man in a blue T-shirt came up and introduced himself.

"Hi, Sean. Tripp Willoughby. We spoke on the phone this morning." Tripp offered a handshake.

"Oh, yeah, about the obedience classes for the therapy pets thing." With a polite smile in Diana's direction, Sean addressed Tripp. "Ready to set up a schedule?"

Diana tamped down a pang of irritation. She stepped forward and extended her own hand. "I'm still recruiting my volunteers," she stated. "I just need some information I can give them about your availability, fees and such."

Sean tugged on the ends of a leather leash dangling from his neck. Clearly getting the message that this was Diana's project, he motioned her toward some offices at the far end of the checkout counters. Tripp seemed to have grasped the point, too, letting Diana lead the way.

Squeezing between a cluttered desk and a tall filing cabinet, Sean shuffled through a drawer and brought out a trifold brochure. "This describes what my four-week basic obedience classes cover. Unless your volunteers want to join one of our nightly classes here at the store, my only availability for off-site training would be Sunday afternoons. You'd just need to arrange for a facility."

Diana nodded thoughtfully. "I'll work on that. Can you tentatively put us on your calendar for the next four Sundays? This all needs to be completed by the first week of November."

"Dr. Willoughby mentioned that." Sean flipped pages in a desk planner and began marking off Sunday afternoons. "Okay, just let me know in the next few days if this is a go."

With sign-up instructions and several of Sean's brochures in hand, Tripp and Diana left the pet store. They hadn't traveled far before Diana's initial optimism faded. "None of this matters if I can't come up with enough dog owners to participate."

Tripp reached across the console to gently touch her hand. "You're not getting discouraged, are you?"

Her first instinct was to pull away, but she realized she didn't want to. She'd forgotten how nice it felt when she and Tripp used to hold hands.

Or maybe she hadn't forgotten at all. As if with a will of their own, her fingers entwined with his. She blinked rapidly, unable to tear her eyes away from the sight of his manly, sun-bronzed hand wrapped so tenderly around her much smaller, paler one.

Tripp slid his hand free and grasped the steering wheel. He cleared his throat roughly. "I mean…it's a worthy cause. Once your recruitment flyers start circulating, you shouldn't have any trouble lining up volunteers."

"I—I hope you're right." Tucking the hand he'd touched firmly into her lap, Diana sat straighter. She'd overreacted, clearly. Tripp had only meant to reassure her, and now they were both fighting embarrassment.

To ease the tension, Diana mentioned how the flyers she'd given out this morning at the doughnut shop had already garnered interest. Besides Kelly, three other customers had said they might be calling for more information.

"There you go," Tripp said, as if her success were a

foregone conclusion. "You'll have the minimum number of sign-ups in no time."

With a shaky smile, Diana turned toward the window. She appreciated Tripp's help and encouragement, but to work this closely with him? She wasn't so sure her heart could withstand the emotional chaos.

Tripp returned Diana to her car behind the doughnut shop, then headed out to his cabin. But all that evening, he couldn't get his mind off the way her hand had felt in his. The moment had seemed so natural, so right.

But also very, very wrong. Much as his heart was urging him to pick up where they'd left off all those years ago, he couldn't rush this. They both needed time to adjust to the "new normal" of being near each other again.

Finishing his first appointment the next morning, he escorted Vince Mussell and his overgrown mutt out to the reception desk. "Darby's vaccines are good for three years," Tripp explained. "Yolanda will give you his new rabies tag, and I'll call in a couple of days with the heartworm test results."

"Thanks, Doc." Vince stroked the dog's big, brown head. "This boy may not be so pretty to look at, but he's a cuddler. He means the world to Janice and me."

"He is a sweetheart." Best guess, Darby was part Labrador, with maybe some shepherd and bloodhound mixed in. "Say, would you and your wife consider volunteering with Darby as a therapy pet? He looks like a good candidate."

Vince's forehead creased. "Therapy pet? What exactly is that?"

Tripp handed Vince one of Diana's flyers. "This will explain. Do you know Diana Matthews?"

"Oh, sure, from the doughnut shop. Sweet girl." A thoughtful frown twisting his lips, Vince perused the flyer. "Hmm, I'll show this to Janice. Looks interesting."

Before the day ended, Tripp had handed out flyers to the owners of every canine patient he'd seen that looked even halfway suitable for Diana's program. He couldn't completely rule out a dog that exhibited extreme nervousness at a veterinary appointment, because the animal might be perfectly fine in less stressful social situations. It would be up to the therapy pets evaluator to make the final decision.

Would it be too soon to let Diana know about the positive responses? He could wait and call after he got back to the cabin, or he could casually drop in at the doughnut shop, using the excuse that he'd like to replenish his supply of the flyers.

The longing to see Diana again, even if only as a friend, won out. Leaving the clinic, he headed into town and parked in front of the doughnut shop, only to be reminded it closed at four. The disappointment forcing the air from his lungs seemed way out of proportion, but he couldn't help himself.

He'd just about accepted the inevitability of not seeing Diana again until tomorrow when his cell phone rang. Diana's name on the display kicked his pulse into high gear. The sensible part of his brain shouted at him to get his eagerness under control before he answered, but he ignored it. "Diana, hi. I was just thinking about—"

"Tripp, I need help." The panic in her voice hit him

like a bucket of ice water. "It's my cat Tiger. I don't know what's wrong."

Professionalism taking over, Tripp tightened his grip on the phone. "What are the symptoms?"

"Retching, coughing, wheezing and he acts like his stomach hurts." Diana gave a shaky sniff. "I'm sorry for bothering you, but the clinic number went to the answering service and I was too scared to wait for a callback."

"It's okay. I'm still in town, and I can head straight back to the clinic. Can you meet me there with Tiger?"

"I'll be there in five minutes."

"Don't rush. Better to be safe—" Too late. The line went dead.

Tripp tossed the phone onto the seat, then backed out of the parking space and aimed his SUV in the direction of the clinic. He suspected Diana's cat had an impacted hair ball, which could be life threatening without immediate treatment.

Arriving at the clinic, he spotted Diana waiting on the front step, her arms wrapped protectively around a bulky blue cat carrier. Tripp parked next to Diana's car, then hurried to unlock the clinic. He showed Diana to the first exam room, where she helped him coax the hefty striped tomcat out of the crate.

A cursory exam reaffirmed Tripp's suspicions. He shared them with Diana. "To be certain, I need to sedate him and get some X-rays. Then we're probably talking surgery."

She nodded and wiped away a tear. "Do whatever you need to."

An hour and a half later, Tripp had successfully removed the obstruction. Knowing Diana would be anxious for news, he found her in the waiting room. "Tiger did great. He's sleeping off the anesthesia. Want to see him?"

"Yes!" She held his forearm in a death grip as he showed her into the surgery suite, where Tiger lay sleeping in a padded kennel. "Oh, my poor kitty," she murmured, stroking his paw. With a glance at Tripp, she asked, "How soon before he can come home?"

"Since you have other cats, it might be better if I kept him here for a few days while the incision heals." At her look of dismay, Tripp added, "I'll take good care of him, I promise."

"I know. It's just that..." Diana covered her mouth to stifle a sob.

Instinctively, Tripp pulled her into his arms—and instantly knew it was a mistake, because holding her like this was bringing back all kinds of memories. As he strove for the wherewithal to release her, she pressed closer, her face buried in the hollow space beneath his collarbone.

Then, just as quickly, she shuddered and pulled away. "Sorry, didn't mean to fall apart like that." Using the back of her hand, she brushed wetness from her cheeks and returned her attention to the cat. "Tiger's been with me the longest of all my pets. If I lost him, I don't know what I'd do."

A coldness seeped in to fill the emptiness Diana had left behind. Finding the breath to speak, Tripp willed calm detachment into his tone. "I told you, he'll be fine. Once he's ready to go home, I'll give you some pointers on how to keep this from happening again."

"Good, thanks." Diana glanced at her watch. "Wow,

is it really after seven? No wonder my stomach's growling."

Caught up in doing his job, Tripp hadn't even thought about food. Now, Diana's reminder brought an answering rumble from his own abdomen. The banana he'd downed for an afternoon snack had long since worn off, but he wouldn't leave the clinic while Tiger was still in recovery. "Go get some dinner. I'll keep an eye on Tiger."

Diana chewed her lip. "Well, I do need to check on my other kids. Can I bring you back something?"

"Thanks, but I'll grab a snack from the fridge. Anyway, don't you have to be up early to open the shop?" Tripp nodded toward the door. "Go home. We'll be fine here."

Halfway down the corridor, Diana halted and spun around. "Tripp?"

"Yeah?"

"Thank you." With a quick but meaningful smile, she hurried out.

One shoulder braced against the door frame, Tripp suppressed a sigh of longing. Every minute he spent in Diana's company only made him want her more. He'd been crazy about her in college, all set to pop the question before…

Nope, not going there. It was no use dwelling on might-have-beens. He'd made a good life for himself in spite of everything, and so had Diana. If—and it was a big *if*—there was still the slightest hope of a future together, their relationship would have to be based on who they were now, not the starry-eyed romantics they'd been twelve years ago.

But would Diana ever be ready to give him—*them*—another chance at love?

Diana had no idea what she would have done if Tripp hadn't answered her panicked call. Doc Ingram, busy as he'd been while running the practice single-handedly, wouldn't have been quite so easy to reach in such an emergency.

Thank You, God. Thank You for sending Tripp back into my life, exactly when I needed him.

Because he was an excellent vet, that's all. Smart and kind and dedicated—

"Face it, girl," she murmured to herself as she spread fresh bedding in Alice's crate, "he's still the same man you fell in love with back in college."

The same…but also different. Different in ways Diana had yet to comprehend. Yes, apparently, he paid a lot more attention to a healthy diet than he ever had when they were together. But he also seemed more mature, more grounded, more…jaded?

No, *jaded* was too strong a word. *Resigned*, maybe, as if making the best of some painful disappointment in his life.

Painful disappointment? Diana slapped her forehead, startling the parakeet. "Sorry, Sparky." She placated him with an apple slice while wondering how Tripp could possibly regret the breakup as much as she did.

He'd been the one to call things off. *He* was the one who, with one cowardly phone call, had destroyed their dreams for a future together.

Turning her attention to preparing supper for the mewing cats circling her ankles, she thrust aside any thoughts of letting Tripp off the hook. There was no argument about his veterinary skills, nor the fact that Diana probably wasn't going to get this therapy pets program off the ground without his help. But she absolutely would not let herself fall for him again.

Right. Like the fool she was, she'd gone all weepy and fallen into his arms. It galled her now to recall how naturally the moment had happened. Until she'd come to her senses anyway.

"Professional," she told Lucinda and Midnight as she set bowls of salmon-flavored cat food in front of them. "I've *got* to keep this relationship strictly professional."

After warming a microwave dinner for herself, Diana carried it to the sofa and flipped on the TV. By the time she finished her meal, both cats had curled up next to her, and since Tiger usually claimed her lap, she missed him all the more. She glanced at her cell phone lying on the end table. Would Tripp mind if she called to check on Tiger?

Deciding Tiger was *her* cat and it didn't matter if Tripp minded—he was a *professional*, after all—she picked up the phone.

"Hi, Diana." His silky-smooth voice sounded cheerful but tired.

And totally discombobulated her. "Hi. I, uh…wondered how Tiger's doing."

"He's still a little groggy but in no pain. I'll make sure he has a restful night."

It only then occurred to Diana that Tripp meant to spend the night at the clinic, and guilt niggled about not taking him some supper. On the other hand, he was probably used to this sort of thing. Still, she couldn't stop herself from asking, "Did you find something to eat?"

He hesitated a couple of seconds too long. "A little."

"What, exactly?"

"Yolanda left some pita chips and hummus in the snack room."

"Tripp! That's not supper." Diana cringed at the upsurge of concern swelling her chest. "You should have let me bring you something."

"I'm a big boy. I'll survive." His tone grew edgy. "You've got enough on your mind. I don't need you worrying about me."

"But I do—" She clamped her mouth shut. *Way to keep it professional, Matthews.* "I mean, if not for me, you'd have had a relaxing evening and a decent meal. I just…feel bad about that."

"Well, don't. As soon as I check Tiger one more time, I'm running over to the supermarket to pick up something and bring it back." A weary laugh sounded in Diana's ear. "This is what I signed up for, Di. I love my work, and I'd do the same for any of my patients."

"Oh." She didn't know whether to feel relieved or offended. Worse, he'd called her Di again, which stirred up all kinds of other emotions she'd rather not deal with. "Well…thank you."

"Get some sleep. I'll call you in the morning with a report."

Clicking off, Diana had a feeling she was in for yet another sleepless night.

She couldn't have been more right. Staring at her reflection in the bathroom mirror the next morning, she wished she could blame her dark circles and bloodshot eyes on worrying about Tiger, because the truth was a lot harder to deal with. During the little sleep she'd gotten, her dreams had been invaded by Tripp—his eyes, his smile, his arms gently enfolding her as she leaned into his solid chest.

"What am I going to do?" she said aloud to the frazzled woman in the mirror. Her life had been humming along perfectly fine until Tripp Willoughby showed up. Now everything was—

She waved her hands in a gesture of futility. No time to sort through it all now. The doughnut shop awaited. And so did a giant-sized mug of supercaffeinated coffee.

Work definitely proved a panacea for getting her mind off Tripp. Temporarily, at least. Once the early birds had been served, Diana returned to her office to catch up on some bookkeeping and paperwork.

A few minutes after nine, the business line rang. "Diana's Donuts, Diana speaking."

"Hi, Diana. It's Yolanda from Ingram Veterinary Hospital. Dr. Willoughby wanted me to let you know how Tiger's doing this morning."

Diana flinched. It didn't get much more professional than having the receptionist do the calling. "Yes, how is he?"

"Just fine. Tiger is eating and drinking well and generally on the mend. Doc says Tiger should be ready to rejoin your little family in another couple of days."

"That's wonderful. Thank you." Closing her eyes briefly, Diana took a quick breath. "And thank Dr. Willoughby, too."

Chapter Six

Juniper Bluff might be a small town, but the animal clinic drew plenty of business from the surrounding area, and Tripp's appointment calendar stayed comfortably full. According to Yolanda, they were also getting several new patients as word spread that Doc Ingram had taken on a partner.

Over his lunch hour on Friday, Tripp took a few minutes to look in on his surgical patients—a neutered Pomeranian, a Lab mix with a benign tumor and of course Diana's cat Tiger. The old tomcat's incision seemed to be healing well, and Tripp decided it would be safe to send him home this afternoon. He started to the front desk to ask Yolanda to make the call, then thought better of it. All week long, he'd taken the coward's way out and had his receptionist report to Diana about Tiger's progress. His convoluted logic had him believing if Diana really wanted to talk to him, she'd say so—or, better yet, show up at the clinic wearing the megawatt smile that had always been his undoing.

He was almost glad she hadn't, because he wasn't

sure how much longer he could hide the feelings her nearness had rekindled.

Their personal issues aside, he wanted to find out where things stood with the obedience classes. If she needed more help recruiting volunteers, he'd gladly step up his own efforts—anything to help her be ready for the early-November evaluation.

With a tight-lipped groan, he backtracked to his office and closed the door. He placed the call on his cell phone, knowing she'd see his name on her cell's display. That way, she could choose to answer...or not.

Three rings later, she picked up. "Hi, Tripp." Shyness, and maybe a teensy bit of accusation, tinged her tone. "It's been a while."

"Yeah, I've stayed pretty busy this week." Technically true, but a lame excuse nonetheless. "Thought you might be ready to take your boy home today."

"Yes, definitely! I'll pick him up as soon as we close this afternoon."

Her burst of enthusiasm made Tripp annoyingly envious of the tabby. "Great. So I'll see you shortly after four?"

"I'll be there." All business again, she continued, "By the way, thanks for referring so many of your patients. I've gotten several inquiries this week."

"I'm glad." He cleared his throat. "Any takers for Sean's obedience class?"

"Possibly. Still need to confirm with some phone calls."

"If I can help..."

"I'll let you know." With a crisp goodbye, she ended the conversation.

Naturally this *would* be the one afternoon when

Tripp didn't have a full slate of appointments. After giving a squirming puppy its first round of vaccinations, then explaining to the new owner of a kitten why investing in a scratching post was a much more humane option than declawing, Tripp had little more to occupy himself than catching up on his veterinary journals.

At long last, four o'clock rolled around. With one eye on the front door, Tripp tried to look busy reorganizing magazines in the reception area while Yolanda completed the daily computer entries and filing.

The superobservant receptionist wasn't fooled, though. "I was going to clock out as soon as I finish up here, but if you need a chaperone, I could stick around." She winked. "Of course, I'd expect to be paid double overtime."

"In your dreams." Giving up his pretense, Tripp folded his arms on the counter. "I can assure you, there won't be anything happening here requiring a chaperone."

"Too bad." Yolanda stood across from him to straighten the three remaining therapy pets flyers. She tapped a violet acrylic nail on Diana's name. "Anyone can see you two were meant for each other. Why you are both fighting it so hard is beyond my understanding."

Mine, too, Tripp didn't say aloud. "Too much water under the bridge. Let's leave it at that."

The rumble of tires on pavement drew Tripp's attention to the front windows. With a threatening glance at Yolanda, he strode to the door and held it open as Diana came up the steps. The cat carrier tucked under one arm, she smiled up at him. It wasn't exactly a thrilled-to-see-you smile, but he'd take it.

"I don't have much time," she said, bustling past him

into the waiting room. "I need to return a call from my Visiting Pet Pals contact."

"No problems, I hope."

"I don't think so. She probably wants to make sure everything is still on track." With a quick greeting to Yolanda, Diana set the cat carrier on the floor next to the counter. She fingered the three remaining therapy pets flyers. "This is all you have left?"

Tripp came up beside her. "I've been meaning to ask you for more, but I kept getting sidetracked."

"Yes," Diana said stiffly, "you mentioned you've been busy."

Yolanda patted several file folders into a neat stack. "These can wait until Monday. I'm calling it a day." She took her purse from a desk drawer and stepped from behind the counter. "Nice seeing you, Diana. Take care!" With a pointed look at Tripp, she reminded him to lock up on his way out.

Moments later, the back door banged. Alone with Diana, Tripp whooshed out a breath. "I guess we should get Tiger so you can be on your way and make that call."

"Right." Diana bent to pick up the carrier at the same moment Tripp did, and their heads bumped. "Oh, sorry!"

"No harm done." Rubbing his forehead, Tripp stepped back and let Diana get the carrier. He showed her down the hall to the room where cats were boarded.

Stepping inside, Diana gave a happy gasp and rushed over to where the stray mother cat and kittens were kenneled. "Oh, look how much they've grown!"

"They're doing great. Won't be long until these little guys are ready for their forever homes." Tripp nodded toward a kennel at the far end of the room. "Tiger's down this way."

As Diana approached, the old cat mewed and rubbed against the mesh. "Aw, glad to see me, fella? I've missed you."

Tripp released the latch, and after Diana had given Tiger some hugs and kisses, he helped her ease him into the cat carrier. "I've got some postsurgical instructions up front for you with notes about hair ball prevention."

Diana grimaced. "I'm sure you've got a hefty bill for me, too."

"No hurry. Talk to Yolanda about it next week." They started toward the front. "Anyway, I figure you qualify for our multi-pet discount."

"No kidding." Reaching the reception area, Diana paused and turned. "I'd better get going. Still need to get my notes in order before I call the Visiting Pet Pals lady."

"You'll let me know how it goes, I hope?" Tripp stepped behind the counter to find Tiger's file and retrieve the information sheets he'd prepared.

Tucking the papers into her purse, Diana gnawed her lower lip. "Actually, with your therapy pets experience, I could probably use your advice and moral support for this conversation. I don't want to give Agnes Kraus any reason whatsoever to deny my application."

Tripp's pulse quickened. "Whatever you need."

After a thoughtful pause, Diana asked, "How do you feel about pizza?"

Tripp did some quick mental calculations about his food intake so far this week. He'd been pretty sensible about his choices, and pizza generally wasn't a problem, provided he skipped the spicy or high-fat toppings.

"I actually love pizza," he said, then offered a crooked grin. "Is this a dinner invitation, perchance?"

"If you're buying." Diana wiggled her brows. "Because after I pay my vet bill, you're going to be a lot richer than I am."

"All right, you're on." Too stunned to question Diana's openness to spending the evening with him, he jotted down the name of the pizza place she suggested. "I'll close up shop here and call in the order. Be at your place around six?"

"Great. See you then."

Later, as Tripp placed the call to order their pizza, he wondered what kind of emotional torture he'd just set himself up for.

With Tiger curled up on the sofa cushion beside her, Diana firmly but lovingly instructed Midnight and Lucinda to give him some space. Once the other cats had settled, one on an armchair and the other on a plush ottoman, Diana spread her notes across the coffee table in preparation for her conversation with Mrs. Kraus.

Seeing everything laid out in front of her—seeing her germ of an idea come to fruition after weeks of dreaming and planning—made everything all the more real.

"It's happening, Tiger," she squealed. "I can't wait for Tripp—"

Tripp? Since when was *he* the first person she thought of sharing this moment with? Fists clenched against her mouth, Diana trembled from the shock of how easily the past had converged on the present. She and Tripp had once shared every joy and disappointment, each one a milestone along their journey toward lasting love…until the final disappointment that had shattered her dreams forever.

The doorbell rang, and Diana jumped. She had to get her feelings under control, or Tripp would see the turmoil written all over her face. Tearing the elastic band from her ponytail, she shook out her hair, then stood and straightened her shirt and jeans. There had been no time to change out of the clothes she'd worn at work all day, and a faint aroma of coffee lingered.

Too bad. This certainly wasn't a *date*, which meant she had no excuse for suddenly being so concerned about her appearance. With a steadying breath, she walked casually to the front door. As she pulled it open, enticing smells of crispy crust and flavorful toppings surrounded her.

And of course Tripp stood there wearing a boyish grin and looking as handsome as ever. "Hi. Hope you like chicken with spinach and artichoke hearts."

"Wow, you went gourmet." Diana showed him into the kitchen. "I've got the oven set on warm. We can eat after I talk to Mrs. Kraus."

"I was hoping to get here in time." Tripp slid the pizza box onto an oven shelf, then straightened to face Diana. He looked as if he wanted to take her hand but at the last second dropped his arms to his sides. "Nervous?"

"A little." She checked her watch and whistled out a breath. "Guess I'd better make that call."

Returning to the sofa and her table full of notes and lists, Diana picked up her cell phone and dialed Agnes Kraus's number. With a tight-lipped glance at Tripp, she put the call on Speaker and laid the phone on the coffee table.

"Good evening, Diana," the woman greeted. "This won't take long. I just need a quick update on your progress."

"I've had a very productive week. Eleven dog owners have expressed interest, and we're working now on the obedience qualifications."

"Excellent. Remember, to complete your chapter certification, we will need copies of the dogs' health records, verification of obedience training and documentation from the assisted-living center stating their agreement to participate."

Tripp was already perusing Diana's checklist. He silently passed it to her.

"Yes, ma'am," she said, scanning the page. "Everything's in process. I've already been in touch with the center, and they're anxious to get the program going."

"Very well, then. Keep me posted, and unless I hear otherwise, I'll see you the second Saturday of November for evaluation and volunteer training."

"Looking forward to it." Saying goodbye, Diana released her pent-up breath.

Tripp gave her knee a quick pat. "You did great."

"Thanks. Crazy, but this is almost more nerve-racking than when I applied for my small-business loan to open the doughnut shop."

"Not crazy when it's something you care so much about."

"I do care. This is all for Aunt Jennie." Diana rose to check on the pizza. "My own grandmother—Aunt Jennie's sister—died before I was born, so she's always filled that spot in my life."

"I remember," Tripp said, following her to the

kitchen. "Your great-aunt's a very special lady. I know how much you love her."

His understanding tone brought a catch to Diana's chest. She cleared her throat. "Guess we should eat this pizza before it turns to rubber. What would you like to drink? I have decaf iced tea, diet cola or lemon-lime."

"Iced tea, please. Point me to the cupboard and I'll get plates."

As Diana filled two glasses, she became acutely aware of Tripp moving around behind her, making himself at home in her kitchen. *This is how it should have been*, a wistful voice whispered in her head, *the two of us, a comfortable, old married couple making a home together.*

She swallowed over the lump in her throat and carried the drinks to the table. Tripp had already served slices of pizza onto their plates. Like the gentleman he'd always been, he pulled out Diana's chair for her—which did nothing to mitigate the cozy, homelike ambience. When he asked if he could offer grace and hesitantly reached for Diana's hand, she said a silent prayer of her own that God would get her through the rest of this evening in one piece.

Focusing on the reason for Tripp's visit might be her only saving grace. They ate in silence for a few minutes, and then Diana said, "Forgot to tell you. I asked Pastor Terry about holding obedience classes at the church, and he got the okay for us to use the back lawn on Sunday afternoons, provided the owners do any necessary cleanups."

Tripp helped himself to another slice of pizza, then slanted his head with a curious look. "It occurred to me that you're making arrangements for all these dog owners to join your program, but you don't have a dog yourself."

"I guess it is kind of weird," Diana said with a laugh. "I love dogs, but cats are a little less demanding. Besides, I don't have a fenced yard, and with the long hours I work at the shop, I'd feel bad leaving a dog cooped up in the house all day."

"Makes sense. And makes me admire you all the more for what you're doing."

Diana's cheeks warmed. "If Aunt Jennie hadn't had to give Ginger away, I'd probably never have gotten involved with this project." Her voice dropping to a murmur, she added, "Nobody should be deprived of that kind of unconditional love and companionship."

"I agree," Tripp said huskily. He stared at his half-eaten pizza slice. "Di…if I could undo the past, make up for how I hurt you—"

"Don't say it, Tripp. We're not going there tonight. And never again, okay?" It was the only way Diana could bear being this close to him. "That was then, this is now, and all that matters is the people we are today."

Tripp slowly lifted his gaze to meet hers, and in the depths of those intense blue eyes, Diana saw something that rocked her to her core. "If you believe that," he began hesitantly, "then do you think we could start over?"

Her heart stammered. "Start over?"

With a tender smile, Tripp took her hand. "Please. Give me a chance to get it right this time."

Nearly choking on her emotions, Diana clutched his hand with both of hers. "You've got to know how scary this is for me. My heart won't survive getting broken again."

A long, slow sigh escaped Tripp's lips. "As far as it's in my power, I promise that won't happen."

His choice of words struck a subtle warning note in Diana's brain, but she was too caught up in the moment to care. This was Tripp, the man she'd fallen in love with all those years ago and still cared for despite all her efforts to put him out of her heart. Could this really be God offering them a second chance at happiness? If so, she couldn't let it slip away.

Tripp was too elated to do or say anything but bask in the moment. The time would come eventually for him to confide in Diana about the Crohn's, but for now, he wanted to just *be*—him and his girl, sharing pizza and conversation, and laying out the plans for her therapy pets project.

Their project. Because he felt more a part of it— more a part of Diana's life—than he'd imagined possible barely three weeks ago.

After clearing away the supper dishes, they moved to the sofa, where they divided up the list of potential volunteers and began placing calls. By eight forty-five, they had six sign-ups for the obedience class. Three other owners said their dogs had already earned basic obedience certificates, and the remaining two on the list had decided the program wasn't right for them.

Diana tapped her pen against her chin. "That leaves us with nine strong possibilities, and we only need eight to qualify with Visiting Pet Pals." She grinned at Tripp. "I think this just might work."

"I *know* it will." Resting against the sofa cushions, Tripp nonchalantly draped his arm along the back. When Diana scooted a fraction of an inch closer, he took it as permission to lower his arm to her shoulders. At first contact, they both stiffened briefly. Diana cast him a nervous glance, then slowly relaxed against him.

This was nice—*too* nice. The warmth spreading through Tripp's chest told him he needed to do the responsible thing and say good-night. Still, he couldn't resist allowing himself a few more minutes of this simple pleasure while his thoughts drifted to a future where having Diana next to him like this was an everyday occurrence.

Hearing Diana's grandfather clock begin its nine o'clock chime, Tripp reluctantly pushed aside the lanky black cat that had crawled onto his lap earlier. "Sorry, Midnight, but I need to go."

Diana sat forward, careful not to disturb Tiger curled up next to her. "Watch out for Alice," she told Tripp with a nod toward the lop-eared rabbit sniffing his shoe.

Tripp reached down to stroke the rabbit's velvety-soft fur. "You should find out if Visiting Pet Pals would accept Alice in the program. The group I worked with during my internship allowed dogs, rabbits, guinea pigs and birds."

"I hadn't thought of that. Next time I talk to Agnes, I'll ask." Diana rose along with Tripp and walked him to the door. "Thanks again for bringing the pizza, and for all your help."

"My pleasure." Tripp paused on the front step, fingers tucked into the pockets of his khakis. Diana looked so beautiful standing there, brown eyes shimmering and her thick, dark hair haloed by the entryway chandelier. He suffered a nearly irresistible compulsion to kiss her but knew it was way too soon for such a move.

Instead, he asked, "I guess you'll be busy tomorrow at the doughnut shop?"

"We close at two on Saturdays, but then I need to catch up on bookkeeping and supply orders."

"And afterward?"

Diana cast him a regretful frown. "I promised Aunt Jennie a visit. As crazy as things have been lately, I haven't gotten by to see her as often as I'd hoped."

"I'm sure she understands. Give her my best, will you? I still remember how sweet she was to me back when…" Grimacing, Tripp left the words unsaid.

After a moment's hesitation, Diana suggested, "Why don't you come along? Aunt Jennie would love to see you again."

Tripp brightened. "Are you sure?"

"So long as you promise not to say anything about our therapy pets project. Remember, I'm planning this as a surprise for Aunt Jennie's birthday next month."

"My lips are sealed." Tripp made a zipping motion across his mouth.

Diana promised to call when she finished work so that Tripp could meet her at the assisted-living center. With more bounce in his step than he'd had three hours ago, he climbed into his SUV for the drive to the cabin.

He'd barely gotten out of town when his cell phone rang. His first thought was that Diana was already calling to say she'd changed her mind about tomorrow—about *everything* they'd said about making a fresh start. He answered without looking at the display. "Hey, Diana, it's fine if you'd rather—"

"Diana?" His sister's surprised laugh collided with his eardrum. "What have I missed here, bro?"

"None of your business." Cringing, Tripp tapped the

speaker icon and set the phone on the console. Then his stomach knotted. When he'd spoken with Brooke a couple of days ago, they'd just brought Mom home from the hospital. *Please, Lord, not another setback.* "What's up? Is Mom okay?"

"That's why I'm calling. Got a few minutes?"

Tripp couldn't tell from Brooke's tone whether her news was good or bad. Either way, he'd rather not risk an accident. "I'm on the road. Hang on while I find somewhere to pull over."

Around the next bend, his headlights swept across the turn-in to someone's ranch. He pulled in at an angle, then shifted into Park. Moving the phone closer, he drew air through tight lips. "Okay, talk to me."

"Don't panic. Mom's still holding her own. It's just—" Brooke's voice trembled. "The doctor says it's time to seriously consider hospice."

The knot in Tripp's belly swelled to boulder-sized. He lowered his forehead to the steering wheel. "That means…"

"Yes, Tripp, Mom's winding down." Brooke heaved a long, weary sigh. "We knew this time would come."

Yeah, but Tripp had prayed it would be much, much later. He straightened and massaged his temple. "What do you need me to do, sis?"

"I've emailed you some information from the hospice people. Look it over and get back to me if you have any questions. And, Tripp?"

"Yeah?"

"Quit beating yourself up about this. It isn't your fault."

A fact he acknowledged intellectually, but it still made him want to punch something.

Brooke's tone softened. "Have you told Diana yet?"

"Not yet."

"You need to. You owe it to her...and to yourself."

"I will. Soon. But we're just now getting closer again—"

"Tripp, really? That's wonderful! *And*," she added sternly, "all the more reason you need to be honest with her about why you broke up."

He wouldn't deny it. "When the time is right—I promise. If this really is our second chance, I'm not going to mess things up."

"You'd better not, because twelve years ago I was really counting on having Diana as a sister-in-law, and now you've got my hopes up again."

"Brooke—"

"I'm serious, Tripp. And just think what this would mean to Mom. You know how much she loved Diana. She'd be over-the-moon thrilled if you two got back together."

Tripp pressed one hand hard against an annoying cramp in his abdomen. "Slow down, okay? Diana's barely stopped looking at me like a bug she'd like to squash. 'Back together' is still a ways off."

"But no longer out of the realm of possibility. That's the main thing."

"If you say so." Headlights flashed in Tripp's side mirror as a vehicle slowed behind him. A right-turn signal indicated the driver planned to turn into the drive where Tripp was parked. "Gotta go, Brooke. I'll take a look at the hospice info and get back to you tomorrow. In the meantime, please don't let on to Mom and Dad about Diana. Let me see where this is going first."

"I hear you. Just don't wait too long."

Not if he could help it—for his mother's sake, certainly. But also because he needed to settle the matter in his own mind and heart.

Chapter Seven

A few minutes after three on Saturday afternoon, Diana phoned Tripp to say she was wrapping things up at the doughnut shop and about to head over to the assisted-living center. He sounded relieved to hear from her…but in a way that suggested he had a million other things on his mind. Now, as he trudged up the front walk, the distant look in his eyes confirmed her suspicions. Something definitely troubled him, and she prayed it wasn't more upsetting news about his mother.

Tripp offered a tired smile as he drew closer. "Hope I didn't keep you waiting long."

"Just got here myself." Diana tilted her head. "If you'd rather not—"

"No, it's fine. I've been looking forward to this." Tripp stepped around her to get the door. "Looks like a nice facility. Has your aunt adjusted well?"

The edge to his voice told her he was forcing small talk. Maybe later he'd tell her what had him so preoccupied. In the meantime, she hoped this visit with Aunt Jennie would cheer him up. "She seems happy enough, except for missing her little corgi." Diana led the way through the lobby. "Remember not to say anything about our project, though."

"Haven't forgotten."

They reached the door to apartment 18C. Diana tapped lightly, then peeked in. "It's me, Aunt Jennie. I brought your favorite cream-filled chocolate doughnuts. And I brought a friend."

"Come in, come in!" Face aglow, her great-aunt sat forward in the blue recliner. "I've been on pins and needles waiting for you, honey. Introduce me to your—" Aunt Jennie's brow furrowed, and then her face lit up in a smile. "Oh, my, Tripp Willoughby, as I live and breathe!"

"Hi, Mrs. Stewart. It's great to see you again. Wasn't sure you'd remember me." Tripp strode forward to give Aunt Jennie a kiss on the cheek.

"Of course I remember you!" Clutching Tripp's hand, Aunt Jennie clucked her tongue. "And what's this 'Mrs. Stewart' business? I've always considered you family." Her pointed glance at Diana said she'd like her great-niece to make it a reality.

Behind Tripp's back, Diana cast Aunt Jennie a raised-brow stare: *Don't you dare make a big deal out of this!*

Her great-aunt returned a smirk that only Diana would recognize as her get-over-yourself look. "Tripp, you and Diana sit here on this end of the sofa so I can hear you better."

"Yes, ma'am, thanks." Tripp motioned for Diana to seat herself nearest Aunt Jennie, then eased onto the cushion next to her.

"Closer, closer," Aunt Jennie urged, waving at Tripp to scoot toward Diana. "I don't want to miss a word of our visit."

When barely an inch separated them, Aunt Jennie sat back with a satisfied smile. Diana, on the other hand, could barely breathe. The doughnuts apparently forgotten, the sprightly little woman plied Tripp with questions about what brought him to Juniper Bluff, how he liked being a veterinarian and if he thought he might settle here permanently—*hint, hint.* Diana should have known Aunt Jennie would be all too anxious to play matchmaker.

Then the conversation turned to Tripp's family. With difficulty he described his mother's failing health, then revealed what his sister had told him on the phone last night.

Diana's heart constricted. "Oh, Tripp." She grasped his hand. "You said it was bad, but I had no idea. I'm so sorry."

"Just the mention of hospice makes it hit home with me." Grief darkened his eyes. He swallowed hard. "My mother is dying, and I've got to accept it."

"But your mother knows the Lord," Aunt Jennie said softly. "Find courage for the present and comfort for what is to come by remembering Jesus is already preparing a place for her in heaven."

Tripp nodded. "Thanks, that helps." Giving Diana's hand a squeeze, he stood. "I should get going. Enjoyed seeing you again, Mrs.—I mean, Aunt Jennie."

"Leaving so soon?" Aunt Jennie motioned him over. "You'll visit again, won't you?"

"Count on it." He bent to offer a goodbye hug.

Diana followed him into the corridor. She wanted so badly to share her own hug with him, to somehow ease his unbearable sorrow. "Tripp, my heart is breaking for you."

He lifted his hand to her face, his palm warm against her cheek. Just as quickly, he dropped his arm to his side. "Don't feel sorry for me. Please. I can stand anything but that."

His sharp gaze sliced through her before he turned and strode away.

"Tripp?" She started after him. "Tripp, don't leave—"

Without looking back, he waved halfheartedly. "I'll see you tomorrow at the obedience class."

Deflated and feeling utterly helpless, Diana returned to her great-aunt's apartment. She slipped inside and leaned weakly against the closed door.

"Your poor young man," Aunt Jennie said. "Should he be alone right now?"

"Maybe not, but he made it pretty clear he'd rather be." With a silent groan, Diana crossed to the sofa and sank down. Why did Tripp find it so hard to let someone share his struggles?

Aunt Jennie reached across to pat Diana's knee. "I still remember how inconsolable you were after he broke things off. Nothing anybody said seemed to help, and you finally told us all to leave you be."

"For all the good it did," Diana replied with a smirk. "You, Mom and Dad were all over me like fleas on a dog."

"Your daddy worried most. Scared him to death that you might do something foolish."

"No kidding. He came up to see me at school and spent nearly a week making sure I didn't decide to drop out." Diana rolled her eyes. "As if! The breakup only made me more determined to get my business degree and do something meaningful with my life."

Aunt Jennie sat back and folded her hands, a smug

look flattening her lips. "You've certainly made a success of Diana's Donuts."

Narrowing one eye, Diana frowned. "Okay, out with
it. There's obviously more you mean to say."

"Only that there's more to life than running a successful business." Aunt Jennie motioned toward the
little white bag Diana had set on the side table. "Speaking of doughnuts, though, I'm about ready for one. Care
to join me?"

Diana could only laugh while thanking the Lord for
her great-aunt's wisdom and humor.

When Diana didn't see Tripp at church Sunday
morning, her concern increased. After leaving Aunt
Jennie's yesterday, she'd been sorely tempted to call
and check on him—or even drive out to Serenity Hills
as she had the evening after the open house.

But perhaps giving him space was the best course
of action for now, for both their sakes. Diana was still
reconciling her softening feelings toward him, especially after Friday night and the unmistakable current
of electricity thrumming between them. His arm around
her shoulder as they sat on the sofa, the look of longing
in his eyes as he'd said goodbye on her front porch—
for a fleeting moment she'd had the feeling he wanted
to kiss her.

It stunned her to realize she would have let him.

Following worship, Diana glanced around again,
hoping she might have missed Tripp's arrival. Spot-
ting Doc Ingram and his family, she casually asked if
they'd heard from him.

Doc Ingram frowned. "Think he might be under the
weather. He's got a standing invitation to Sunday din-

ner at our house, but he called earlier to say he couldn't make it."

Seth and Christina Austin, leaving the sanctuary with their two children, strode over. "Asking about Tripp?" Seth said. "I saw him this morning. Seemed okay, just kind of distracted."

Christina touched Diana's arm. "You look worried. Is there something we should know?"

"Tripp's mother is very ill." Diana hoped he wouldn't mind her mentioning it.

"I'm so sorry," Christina said. "He'd mentioned she wasn't in the best of health but didn't give us any details. Has she taken a turn for the worse?"

As briefly as possible, Diana related what Tripp had told her about Mrs. Willoughby's battle with kidney disease. "It looks like they're going to put her in hospice care. Tripp's taking it pretty hard."

By now, Diana's parents had joined the group. Her dad cast her a questioning glance, obviously wondering why Diana suddenly seemed to have the inside track on what was happening in Tripp's life. "You two must be seeing an awful lot of each other lately," he said.

Diana winced. Things had been happening a little too fast to keep her parents in the loop. "Um, yes, Tripp's been helping me with the therapy pets program."

"Has he, now?" Dad arched a brow.

"I was thrilled to hear about your program," Christina said. "If not for getting ready to have twins," she added with a loving smile for Seth, "I'd consider volunteering with Gracie."

"You and Gracie actually helped inspire me," Diana said. As time had passed since her accident, Christina didn't depend on the golden retriever quite as heavily as she once did, but Gracie remained a special part of the Austin family.

As everyone said their goodbyes, Diana's mother linked arms with her. "So you and Tripp are spending more time together? Hmm, I think you'd better come to lunch with us and fill us in."

Getting the third degree from her parents was the last thing Diana needed today, but she didn't see any chance of escape. Determined to get it over with as painlessly as possible, she agreed to meet them at Casa Luis. The after-church crowd typically packed the popular Mexican restaurant, which meant Diana could count on the noise level to keep Mom and Dad from getting too personal with their questions.

Because if they asked point-blank whether she was falling in love with Tripp Willoughby all over again, she wasn't sure how she'd respond.

Tripp pulled into the church parking lot at ten minutes before three. He drove around back, nearer to where the obedience class would be held, and glimpsed Diana talking with Sean, the trainer. Four or five dog owners chatted among themselves while their dogs got better acquainted.

Shutting off the engine, Tripp hauled in a steadying breath. He was doing a little better emotionally than he had been yesterday, when he'd left the assisted-living center so abruptly. Though he'd skipped church this morning, he'd spent a lot of time reading his Bible and trying to pray. Not easy while he still felt so at odds with God over the course his life had taken.

Well, except for one important aspect, and she'd

just looked his way, her smile a beacon of welcome…
and hope.

With a hesitant smile of his own, Tripp ambled over.
He nodded at Diana, then offered his hand to the dog
trainer. "Good to see you again, Sean. Thanks for doing
this."

"Glad it worked out." Sean held the leash of a well-
behaved boxer mix. "This is Brutus, my teaching assistant."

Two more dog owners arrived, including the Mus-
sells with their friendly mutt, Darby. Diana introduced
everyone to Sean, then turned the class over to him. She
motioned Tripp to a nearby bench, where they could sit
and observe.

"Looks like everyone showed up," Tripp commented.

"And they're all so enthusiastic." Diana's shoulders
heaved with a grateful sigh. "Almost wish I had a dog
so I could join the fun."

"Me, too. Maybe after I get a place of my own…"

She tilted her head, the sparkle in her big brown
eyes warming him. "So Juniper Bluff is growing on
you, huh?"

"Guess so."

"I'm glad." Diana braced her elbow on the bench
back, head resting upon her fingertips as she gazed up
at him. "Missed you at church this morning. I prayed
for you…and your mom."

"Thanks. Sorry about yesterday. I was still in a really bad place."

"You don't have to apologize. I can't even imagine
how hard this is for you."

In more ways than one, he didn't say. "Being with
you, though—" His mouth went dry, and he couldn't

finish the thought. He shifted to face her and cupped her elbow with his hand. "Diana, is this really happening? You, me…us?"

"I don't know." Her voice fell to a whisper. "Do you want it to?"

"Do you?"

"I never thought I'd say this, but…yes." Lifting her head, she slid her hand along his arm. When her fingers grazed his cheek, the gentleness of her touch made him shiver. "Can we get back what we had, Tripp? Is it even possible?"

"I'd like to find out." Angling his head, he leaned closer.

Suddenly a pair of giant-sized brown paws plopped on Tripp's lap, and he jerked aside. Instead of the kiss he'd almost shared with Diana, he suffered Darby's long, wet tongue lashing across his face.

Diana laughed out loud as Tripp grabbed the hairy beast's drooling muzzle with both hands. "Hey, big boy," he said through his own laughter, "enough is enough!"

"Sorry, Doc!" Vince Mussell jogged over and grabbed Darby's dangling leash. "Guess we have more work to do on the 'stay' command."

"Practice makes perfect." Tripp patted Darby's rump as Vince coaxed the dog toward the other class members.

Still snickering, Diana found a tissue in her purse and handed it to Tripp. "You might want to clean up a bit."

It would take more than a flimsy tissue to wipe away that much dog slobber. Until Tripp could wash his face with soap and water, he could kiss goodbye any further thoughts of kissing Diana.

Which was probably for the best. Number one, they were sitting here in plain view of several townsfolk, some of whom might take great pleasure in spreading the word that Juniper Bluff's doughnut lady was making time with the new veterinarian.

Number two? It didn't matter that Tripp had once been on the verge of proposing marriage to the woman he loved. Their breakup had been a cruel one, thanks to his cowardice, and he had a lot to make up for. Even if Diana did seem willing to try again—which thrilled him beyond imagining—his personal life was currently in too big a mess. He had no idea when he might get that dreaded call from Brooke about their mother, and stressing over it wasn't doing his own health any good.

And he simply couldn't bring himself to lay all these concerns on Diana, not when things were going so well between them.

On Monday morning, Tripp discovered the Juniper Bluff rumor mill was alive and well. Doc Ingram had stopped by Diana's Donuts for coffee on his way to the clinic. He wore a mischievous grin as he set a to-go cup and a pastry bag on Tripp's desk. "Heard you and your sweetie were canoodling behind the church yesterday."

"That's a bit of a stretch." Heat rose along the sides of Tripp's neck. "We were just talking, that's all."

"*You* may have thought you were just talking, but half the town is already planning your wedding."

Groaning, Tripp set his elbows on the desk and palmed his eye sockets. "You got all this from picking up coffee and doughnuts?"

Robert plopped into the chair across from Tripp. He opened the bag, pulled out a paper-wrapped glazed doughnut and passed it to Tripp. "Here, drown your sorrows in sugar. Coffee's yours, too. I remembered the soy milk."

"Thanks, you're all heart." Stomach issues notwithstanding, Tripp was mortified enough that he couldn't stop himself from indulging in a little sugar-and-caffeine therapy.

"So," Robert began, taking a sip of his own coffee, "want to tell me what's really going on with you and Diana? The most I've gotten from you so far is that you knew each other in college, but something tells me there's a lot more to the story."

After two delicious but ill-advised bites, Tripp laid aside the doughnut. It was well past time to level with his partner, and maybe it could serve as the next logical step in moving toward full disclosure with Diana. "We were this close to getting engaged," he said, holding his thumb and forefinger millimeters apart. "But I was under a lot of stress at vet school, and the next thing I knew, I landed in the hospital."

Robert offered a grim nod. "The pressure can be rough—haven't forgotten. Was that what kept you from proposing?"

"I could have handled the pressure. What I *couldn't* handle was my diagnosis." Tripp lifted his coffee cup to his lips, then set it down without drinking. He met Robert's gaze. "I have Crohn's disease."

A noisy exhalation whooshed from Robert's lungs. "Wow. I'd never have guessed—although I have noticed you're pretty selective about what you eat." With a guilty glance toward the doughnut, he added, "Sorry if I contributed to the problem."

"It's okay." Tripp released a weak chuckle. "I've kept things pretty much under control for several years now."

"So your disease is what came between you and Diana?" Robert shook his head. "That's not the Diana Matthews I know."

"It wasn't her. I broke things off. Back then, I could barely deal with the diagnosis myself, let alone what it could mean for my future. I couldn't inflict all that on Diana."

Sitting forward, Robert pinned Tripp with a hard stare. "You never told her, did you?"

"I didn't know how." He closed his eyes briefly. "Still don't."

"Well, if things are getting serious again between you two…"

"I know. Believe me, I know."

A knock sounded on Tripp's door, and Yolanda peeked in. "Your first patient is here."

"Thanks, be right there." Tripp stood, as did Robert. "You'll keep this conversation between us?" he murmured to his partner.

"Just don't wait too long."

"Hey, Di," her not-so-favorite customer LeRoy hollered from across the shop. "Or should I be callin' you the future Mrs. Doc Willoughby?"

Diana tried not to cringe. It was turning into a busier Monday than usual, and this kind of banter had been going strong all morning. Not *quite* as vocally as LeRoy, thank goodness.

She carried the coffee carafe to his table and refilled his mug. "Now, LeRoy, you know I don't kiss and tell."

Not that there had actually been a kiss, but they'd

come close. And now it seemed the entire town knew about it.

Seth Austin had just walked in the door. He ambled over, a mile-wide grin splitting his face. "What's this I hear about some kissing going on?"

Diana glared. "*Nobody's* kissing *anybody*."

She set the carafe on LeRoy's table with a thud, then pulled out the chair opposite him. Carefully stepping onto the seat, she stood tall and shouted for attention. "Thank you all *so* much for your continued patronage. But the very next person who says one word about the kiss that *didn't* happen, or so much as hints about my marriage prospects, will be banned from this establishment for life."

Catcalls and applause broke out, a clear indication that no one took her seriously. Not that she expected them to—many of them, including Seth, had known her since childhood and probably felt they had as much of a stake in her future as her own family—but if she didn't at least try to establish some boundaries, she'd never hear the end of this.

The door chime sounded, announcing the arrival of another customer. All eyes turned toward the front, and the room immediately fell silent.

Tripp stood in the doorway, looking temporarily disoriented to find everyone's focus on him. He glanced around uneasily, his gaze finally settling on Diana, still high above the crowd on her makeshift pedestal. One eyebrow arching skyward, he cocked his head. "Did I miss something?"

Almost as one, Diana's customers returned to their previous conversations, acting as if nothing had happened. Diana climbed down from the chair, straightened her apron and held her head high as she marched to her station behind the counter. She would *not* give her patrons the satisfaction of seeing her pay Tripp any more attention than she would any other customer.

By the time she reached the cash register, Tripp stood across the counter from her. "What can I get for you?" she asked with a tense smile.

"How about a Greek yogurt and a bottle of spring water?" With a quick glance over his shoulder, Tripp murmured, "Any chance you could take a short break?"

She nodded. "I'll get Kimberly to cover for me. Wait for me at the gazebo."

After filling Tripp's order, she gave him a couple minutes' head start, then slipped into the kitchen to call Kimberly to the front.

Kimberly snickered. "Does this have anything to do with a certain veterinarian who just stopped in?"

Diana rolled her eyes as she hung up her apron. "I'll be back in fifteen minutes."

She briefly considered using the rear exit, but then she'd have to walk all the way down the alley and around the block. Might as well run the gauntlet since it wouldn't take her customers long to figure out her destination. Ignoring their stares, she headed out to the square.

As she joined Tripp on the bench inside the gazebo, he offered a shy grin. "Awkward, huh? Robert told me things were getting crazy over here. I had a little time between appointments and wanted to make sure you're okay."

She shrugged. "I'm used to the Juniper Bluff busybodies. Sorry you're getting initiated so soon."

"Guess it was inevitable." Tripp swallowed his last

spoonful of yogurt, then tossed the container into a nearby trash receptacle. With a bemused laugh, he asked, "So what exactly were you doing up on that chair?"

"Threatening the busybodies with expulsion." Looking across the street, Diana glimpsed two tiers of peering faces lining her shop windows. She nudged Tripp's arm and nodded toward the onlookers. "Obviously, my words had no effect."

"Obviously." Chuckling, Tripp gave his head a brisk shake. Then, turning serious, he covered Diana's hand with his own. "How would you feel about *really* giving them something to talk about?"

Her heart thumped against her rib cage. "What did you have in mind?"

"I don't know…maybe the kiss we never quite got around to yesterday?"

"You mean right here? In the town square?"

"I promise, I've washed my face since Darby so rudely interrupted us." Tripp's eyes held hers. "Shaved extra close this morning, too."

"Why?" she said, barely able to breathe. "Were you already planning this moment?"

"Not consciously. But I haven't forgotten how you used to complain when my whiskers got scratchy."

"I never did care for the permanent five-o'clock-shadow look."

"Di…" His Adam's apple made a long, slow journey up and down his throat. "I really want to kiss you. Right now. In front of everybody."

She shivered. "Okay, then."

So he did.

Chapter Eight

I kissed Diana!

Even better, she'd kissed him back. Willingly, tenderly, as if the breakup and the intervening years had been wiped away in an instant. It didn't matter that half the town had looked on. It didn't matter that ten minutes later they had to say goodbye and return to their jobs.

All that mattered was not messing up this chance to win back the woman Tripp had once walked away from.

He practically floated back to the clinic. The pet owners he saw at his next appointments probably wondered why Doc Willoughby couldn't seem to stop grinning—even at the end of the day, when Sue Ellen Jamison returned with Cleopatra for another dose of worm medication.

"We may need to change Cleopatra's flea prevention," Tripp explained as he pressed a tissue to his bleeding left index finger. "Is she outside much?"

"Only in the backyard," Sue Ellen said, then sheepishly added, "although she does like to catch birds."

Thus ensued a lengthy conversation about the likely sources of Cleopatra's tapeworm infestation. At first shocked, then remorseful, Sue Ellen peppered Tripp with questions until he pointedly handed her an informative brochure, then ushered her and the ill-tempered cat out to the front and turned them over to Yolanda.

After hanging up his lab coat, scrubbing his hands and applying an adhesive bandage to his wounded finger, he collapsed in his office chair and phoned Diana. "How was the rest of your day? Any fallout from our rendezvous in the gazebo?"

"Nothing I couldn't handle. How about you?"

"Thought the day would never end so I could talk to you again." Hearing Yolanda shutting things down, Tripp lowered his voice. "I was hoping maybe I could take you to dinner."

"Sounds nice. But…maybe we could drive over to Fredericksburg?"

"Where there's a smaller chance of running into anyone we know?" Tripp chuckled. "Good plan. Can I pick you up at six?"

"I'll be ready."

Tripp had just enough time to rush out to the cabin and freshen up. Arriving at Diana's, he let out a low whistle when she answered the door. Her dark waves skimmed the shoulders of a gauzy aquamarine tunic top that complemented her coloring beautifully. Combined with skinny indigo jeans, strappy sandals and silver hoop earrings peeking from beneath her hair, the effect was entrancing.

Helping her into his SUV, Tripp waited till the last possible second before releasing her hand—and only after she cast him a dubious stare. On the drive over to Fredericksburg, she suggested a few of her favorite restaurants, and he chose one he thought most likely to accommodate his dietary restrictions. His insides were still talking back after the two bites of glazed doughnut he'd stupidly ingested that morning.

The restaurant offered a homey atmosphere, and the quiet corner booth where the hostess seated them made it easy to talk. And they talked plenty, long after the dishes were cleared away. Tripp had so many questions about Diana's family, what she'd done immediately after finishing college, where she'd gotten the idea for Diana's Donuts, how each of her pets had found its way into her life.

In turn, he answered her questions about his first years in veterinary practice and what his sister, Brooke, had done after getting her marketing degree, but he deliberately sidestepped any mention of his condition. Crohn's disease wasn't exactly pleasant dinnertime conversation, and he wouldn't put a damper on what essentially amounted to their first real date since college.

The date ended on Diana's front step with a good-night kiss that Tripp had been waiting for all day. Memorizing the way Diana's brown eyes glistened beneath the porch light, he murmured, "Can we do this again soon?"

"Come over after work sometime and I'll fix dinner. How about Wednesday?" Her fingertips rested lightly against the hollow of his shoulder. "Afterward, we can watch a movie…or just talk."

"I'll be here."

On Wednesday, though, Tripp had to cancel when an emergency appointment kept him at the clinic until late in the evening. Someone had come upon a stray dog that had been hit by a car, but the injuries were too severe, and Tripp ultimately had to euthanize the poor animal. No matter how many times he'd been through that, it never got easier. He went home exhausted and with his stomach in knots.

Then he phoned Diana, and just hearing her voice soothed away the stress. After the call, he fell asleep imagining coming home to Diana every evening and sharing the day's highs and lows. "It is not good for the man to be alone," Scripture said, and Tripp was coming to believe it as he never had before.

He'd just told Diana good-night and was ready to crawl into bed when his phone rang with a call from Brooke. He squeezed his eyes shut briefly before answering. "Hey, sis."

Her tremulous exhalation sounded in his ear. "We had our first visit from the hospice nurse today."

His heart plummeted. Everything happening this week had helped to distract him from worries about his mother. "How'd it go?"

"She's very professional but also extremely kind and caring. We all liked her."

"And Mom? How's she taking it?"

"She's reached the point of acceptance." Brooke sniffled. "A lot faster than the rest of us, I'm afraid."

Tripp didn't doubt it. "I still wish I could help somehow."

"I know you do. But we're coping. The nurse will come every morning, and I've arranged my work schedule so I can get home earlier each day to help ease the strain on Dad."

"So…no more dialysis?"

Another shuddering breath. "No, Tripp. No more dialysis."

He didn't have to ask what that meant. "Dear God,"

he began, struggling for the strength to pray but unable to find the words. How did anyone pray in a situation like this? For a miracle of healing, for a few more weeks or months to say their goodbyes…or for death to come quickly and peacefully?

"Mom's doctor says she shouldn't be in any pain, so that's a comfort," Brooke said. "Mostly she'll just have less and less energy as things wind down."

Tripp pinched the bridge of his nose. "You'll let me know if it looks like I should come before Thanksgiving?"

"I promise. But Mom's already making plans for having all of us with her for the holiday, so you know she'll fight to hang on for all she's worth." A tear-filled laugh burbled from Brooke's throat. "She even had me pull out her recipe box the other day so I could start on the shopping list."

"That's our mom," Tripp said, shaking his head.

But the realization that this could be the last Thanksgiving he ever spent with his mother hit Tripp hard. After the call ended, he sat on the edge of his bed for several long minutes while his emotions ran rampant. If only he could hear Diana's voice again…

He dialed her number. Then, noticing it was nearly 11 p.m., he immediately disconnected. As early as Diana had to be at the shop in the morning, she was probably sound asleep already.

A second later his phone rang—Diana. "Tripp? Did you just call?"

"Sorry if I woke you. Didn't notice how late it was."

"Is everything okay?" Concern overshadowed the grogginess in her voice.

He told her about the call from Brooke. "I shouldn't

have bothered you, but after the day I had, and then this—" His voice broke.

"No, no, I'm glad you called." She paused. "I hate that you're alone out there. Do you want to come over? I can make us a late-night breakfast, and we can watch old reruns on TV to help get your mind off things."

Tempted as he was, he wouldn't disrupt Diana's rest any more than he already had. "I feel better just talking to you. These past few days...they've meant so much."

"For me, too, Tripp." Sincerity laced her tone. "And please, never, ever hesitate to call or come over anytime you need to talk. What your family's going through—I can't even imagine how hard it must be to watch someone you love deal with such a devastating illness."

Thanking her for listening, Tripp told her to get some sleep and said good-night. A twinge in his belly reminded him he'd forgotten to take his nightly medications, but as he stood at the bathroom sink with a pill bottle in one hand and a glass of water in the other, Diana's parting words penetrated.

When, if ever, could he bear to burden her with the possibility, no matter how remote, that his own disease could turn devastating? His doctors had prepared him for the various complications he could face, the worst of which involved extensive surgery and potentially traumatic lifestyle changes—adjustments Tripp couldn't imagine forcing on someone he loved.

And yet, a future without Diana scared him even more.

On Thursday, Diana phoned Tripp during the late-morning lull, catching him between appointments. "Any chance we could meet for lunch?"

"Sounds nice, but…another time, maybe? I've got to get some lab samples ready to send out." His tone suggested he was glad to hear from her, but he also seemed distant, distracted. Between work and family concerns, he had every right to be.

Still, Diana couldn't shake the feeling that he held something back, as if he regretted being so open with her on the phone last night. Was it only his natural reserve? Or had they tried too quickly to pick up the pieces of their relationship, and now he was having second thoughts? "Sure," she said, trying hard to sound upbeat. "Call me anytime."

She didn't hear from him again for two long days. In the meantime, she second- and third- and fourth-guessed exactly where this thing between them was headed.

On Saturday afternoon, as Diana and her crew wiped tables and straightened up before closing, Tripp walked in.

With a knowing smile, Kimberly relieved Diana of the broom and dustpan she'd been wielding. "Get going. I'll finish up and shut things down."

Hands perspiring for no obvious reason, Diana shrugged out of her apron as she strode over to greet Tripp. "Hey, stranger."

He looked as uneasy as she felt. "Sorry I haven't been in touch."

"I've been worried." *And not just about your mom.*

Tripp glanced around the shop, where Kimberly and two other workers bustled about. "Can we go somewhere?" he asked softly. His crooked smile turned wistful. "I've missed you."

Five minutes later, they sat in the gazebo, Diana's

hand locked firmly in Tripp's and her heart hammering like that of a lovesick teenager. He hadn't said a word since they'd started across the street. Now, deep crevices etching the corners of his eyes, he stared at the scuffed floorboards.

"Tripp," Diana whispered, "what is it?"

"Just a lot on my mind, that's all."

She chewed her lip, a desperate ache squeezing her heart. "Maybe you should just pack up and go to California. Spend this time with your mom while you can. Doc Ingram would understand. Everybody would."

He gave his head a small shake. "No, I can't turn my back on my responsibilities here. Anyway, as Brooke keeps reminding me, Mom could—" A guttural sound choked off his words. He cleared his throat. "She could linger for weeks yet."

"But still—"

"Brooke will let me know if I need to fly out sooner than later. Until then, I just need to keep busy."

Diana nodded in understanding, all the while wishing she had any clue what to do to make things better. She suggested the first thing that came to mind. "Want to come over later? I could make us a light supper."

"Thanks, but I think I'll head home. I've got some veterinary journals I need to catch up on." Then, as if realizing how distant he sounded, he dipped his chin and sighed. "I'm sorry, Di. With everything I'm dealing with, I wouldn't be very good company."

"That doesn't matter to me. We don't have to talk at all if you don't want to. I just—" She released a sharp sigh and pressed his hand between hers. "I just want to help."

"I know," he said, barely meeting her gaze, "and I'm

not purposely shutting you out. I'm just trying to work through some stuff."

"I get that you're worried about your mom. But is it more than that?" Diana held her breath. "Is it…us?"

His grimace said it all.

Rising, she stood in front of him, arms locked at her waist. "It was all too easy, wasn't it? Falling back into the past and pretending like—"

Tripp shoved to his feet. His hands clamped hard around her shoulders. "There's no pretending here, Di. I'm still in love with you. I want us to be together as much as—no, even *more* than I did twelve years ago."

"Then why do you keep pulling away?" She searched his face but found no answers there, only those dusky blue eyes clouded with pain and uncertainty.

His gaze drifted toward the ceiling briefly before he drew her back to the bench. Leaving a few inches of space between them that felt like the Grand Canyon, he sat forward with his hands clasped between his knees. "You're right, it was way too easy slipping back into what we had, and now I'm scared to death of jumping into something neither of us is ready for."

Diana's fingertips curled around the edge of the bench. "I think I'm finally getting the picture. Basically you're telling me you're a commitment-phobe." Jaw clenched, she slowly shook her head. "All the signs were there. I should have figured this out years ago."

"Maybe you're right." Tripp straightened with a tired sigh. "But not for the reasons you think."

"Care to explain, then?" She couldn't mask the bitterness in her tone.

He glanced at her, his lips parted as if he was about to reply. Then his breath caught and he looked away.

"Okay, fine." Diana stood once more. "If you don't have the guts to be honest with me, I've got plenty of other ways to spend my Saturday afternoon."

Before she'd taken three steps, Tripp caught her and whirled her around, trapping her lips in a kiss that rocked her to her toes. When the kiss ended, they both stood breathless. Tripp drew her close and rested his head on hers. "I want to explain things, believe me. But I'm not thinking straight, and until I get through this thing with my mom, I can't trust myself not to hurt you…or mess things up even worse than before."

"You can't mess things up, not if you really love me." Diana moved toward him, arms outstretched. "Let me help you through this."

He accepted her embrace with a shuddering exhalation. "You already are, just by being here."

She tipped her head. "Then why doesn't it seem like enough?"

His gaze locked with hers for a searing moment before he lifted his head and took a purposeful step back. He dropped his arms to his sides. "I have to go, Di. Just please, don't give up on me."

"I won't," she murmured. But as he slipped past her down the steps, a tremor shook her insides, a certain, terrifying sense that she was on the verge of losing him again.

On Sunday afternoon, Diana sat alone on one of the benches on the church lawn to watch the obedience class. Tripp hadn't shown up yet, and though he hadn't exactly said he'd be there, she couldn't stop worrying. He'd seemed so conflicted and confused yesterday, and then had hardly spoken five words to her at church that morning, just hurried out to his car as soon as worship ended.

After checking her cell phone one more time to see if she'd missed a text or call, she made up her mind to drive out to the cabin as soon as the class ended. He might be holding her at arm's length, but his reticence was no match for her determination.

Forty minutes later, Sean ambled over with his boxer, Brutus. "Everyone's coming along real well."

"Wonderful." Rising, Diana forced a smile. "Do you think two more Sundays will have them ready?"

"Don't see why not. A couple of dogs still need to work on some skills, but if the owners keep up the practice between classes, they should be okay."

Encouraged, Diana chatted briefly with the owners. All seemed enthusiastic about earning their dogs' obedience certificates and passing Agnes Kraus's evaluation. Diana reminded them about the veterinary forms they'd need to provide before the group could be authorized as a Visiting Pet Pals chapter.

"No Doc Willoughby today?" Vince Mussell tugged on Darby's leash to stop him from sniffing a piece of trash.

"He's dealing with some serious family concerns. His mother isn't well." Diana glanced away briefly while composing her expression into something resembling a smile. "I know he would have been here if he could."

"Well, I hope everything turns out okay. Sure like that fella. Darby does, too." Vince scratched the dog behind the ears. "Yep, Doc Willoughby has a real nice way about him."

Diana couldn't agree more.

Then Tripp's warm baritone sounded behind her. "My ears were burning. Y'all talking about me?"

She swung around and came face-to-face with his hesitant half grin. "Tripp. I didn't think you were coming."

"Meant to. Went to my office this afternoon to catch up on a few things, then got on the phone with my mom and dad. We talked for so long that I lost track of time." He handed Diana a manila envelope. "Hoped I'd catch you before you left. I made copies of vaccination records and wrote up the health assessments you'll need for the evaluation."

Diana narrowed her eyes as she accepted the envelope. "You did all this today?"

"Just keeping busy." Tripp cast a polite nod at Vince and reached down to scratch Darby behind the ears. "This guy doing okay with his lessons?"

"Better than last week," Vince said with a snort, "but we still have some work to do. Good to see you, Doc. Heard about your mom. Janice and I will keep y'all in our prayers."

"Appreciate it."

Diana reached out to touch Tripp's arm. She'd rather hug him, but taking in Tripp's detached expression, she thought better of it. Plus, Vince was standing right there. Instead, she quietly asked, "How's your mother doing today?"

"About the same. Holding her own." With a brisk nod, Tripp returned his attention to Vince and his dog. "What exactly is Darby having trouble with? Any way I can help?"

Clearly, Tripp was heavily into avoidance mode.

Crossing her arms, Diana stepped aside while Vince described Darby's training weaknesses.

"Biggest problem is he's a puller," Vince explained. "Can't get him to walk nicely beside me on the leash."

Frowning, Tripp scratched his chin, then knelt in front of the dog. He unsnapped the leash, flipped it around to the loop handle and wove it into a figure eight, which he fitted over Darby's neck and snout as a makeshift halter. "Try this," he said, handing the other end to Vince. "It'll give you more control in leading him."

Vince gave Darby the command to heel, then stepped out. The dog started to pull ahead, but the halter immediately drew his attention back to his master. He slowed his pace and trotted alongside Vince with new respect.

"Wow," Vince said, grinning over his shoulder as he led Darby in a broad circle. "You should be teaching this class, Doc. Any other quick tips?"

"The main thing is consistency. Just keep practicing every day. And lots of long walks. That'll burn off some of Darby's energy so he's more ready to focus on the training."

Burning off energy. Sure seemed Tripp was doing more of that himself. Diana wondered what it would take to reclaim his focus on their relationship.

Tripp had never felt so torn. He'd seen the look in Diana's eyes and sensed how much she wanted to reach out to him, to hold him and comfort him. Yet so much still stood between them, and he was way too close to blowing his second chance to have her back in his life permanently.

His brain kept replaying the phone conversation with

his parents earlier. Dad had sounded so much older than the last time they'd talked, and when his dad had stepped away from the phone for a moment, Tripp had said as much to his mom.

Caring for an invalid will do that to you, Mom had said. *He's worn out, and so am I. Soon we'll both be able to rest.*

Those softly spoken words had nearly undone Tripp. All he could say was, *I'm sorry. I'm so, so sorry.*

And Mom had kept telling him he had nothing to be sorry about. Not one thing. *Let's talk about happy news*, she'd said. *Tell me more about your life in Juniper Bluff. Tell me more about Diana. I always did like that girl. She had spunk.*

Still does, and plenty of it, Tripp thought now as he and Diana walked out to the parking lot together...close but not touching.

He'd sidestepped any hints to his parents about the possibility of getting back together with Diana. Those first few weeks in Juniper Bluff, he hadn't held much hope. But now, painfully aware of what his mother's illness was doing to Dad—to all of them—he had even less.

"Gotta go," he said as they reached Diana's car. He opened her door for her. "Talk to you soon."

"I hope so." With one hand on the door frame, she clasped his hand. Before he could resist, she tugged him close for a goodbye kiss.

Her featherlight touch froze him to the spot. Jaw firm, he watched her drive away before climbing into his own car. But instead of heading home, he returned to the clinic. He sat down at his desk and dove into a stack of files and other paperwork that could easily have waited until Monday morning.

My grace is sufficient for thee...

The scripture he'd relied on so often whispered through his thoughts.

My grace...sufficient...

He closed the file he'd been reading, leaned back in his chair and took several long, slow breaths. And remembered what his dad had said on the phone this afternoon, *One day at a time, son. Only choice we have is to take this one day at a time.*

That's what Tripp had to do, too. He was smart enough to realize he was way too vulnerable these days—*not* the ideal frame of mind to make any radical decisions about his future. Especially where Diana was concerned. Like his dad, he needed to take each day as it came and make the best of it.

In the meantime, he'd pray that God would somehow show him—one way or the other—whether keeping Diana in his life was the right thing to do.

Chapter Nine

Diana didn't see much of Tripp the following week. He'd called on Tuesday but said he was between appointments and couldn't talk long. He hadn't sounded quite so distant, though, which eased Diana's mind. She could relate to his need to keep himself occupied—until he'd come back into her life a few weeks ago, she'd had plenty of practice herself.

But it didn't make being apart any easier.

On Wednesday, she invited him over for supper, and he surprised her by accepting. They spent a relaxed evening together, mostly talking about who had stopped in at the doughnut shop, Tripp's most interesting veterinary case of the day and—of course—the therapy pets program. When Diana asked Tripp about his mother, his simple reply was, "Not much change."

They spoke on the phone a few more times over the next couple of days, and on Saturday afternoon, Diana persuaded Tripp to go on a horseback ride with her. Rather than risk a replay of Mona's feistiness, she asked Seth if they could take out a couple of his calmer trail horses.

Out on the trail, it was as if Diana could see the tension melting from Tripp's shoulders. As they arrived in the clearing at the top of the hill, he reined his horse to a halt and looked up at the cloudless blue sky.

"I needed this," he said, then turned to her and smiled his special smile, the one that never failed to convey how much he loved her.

She grinned back, glad for the sunglasses to hide the wetness filling her eyes. "You know what they say. All work and no play…"

"Makes Doc Willoughby a very strung out, self-absorbed, inattentive boyfriend." His mouth twisted in an apologetic frown, but Diana took heart at the fact that he'd actually referred to himself as her boyfriend.

"No more doom and gloom, Doc Willoughby. Today's all about having fun." Diana nudged her horse closer, until the two horses were parallel. She scanned the far side of the meadow. Then, with a mischievous glance at Tripp, she pointed to a tall, skinny cedar. "Race ya to that tree. Loser buys dinner."

Before he could react, she kicked her horse into motion. Not that it did much good, since these trail horses rarely moved faster than a bone-crunching trot.

"No fair!" Tripp shouted behind her, but she heard the laughter in his voice. A couple of seconds later he caught up and even passed her.

She decided right then to let him win. He'd already won back her heart anyway—something she'd never have believed possible if anyone had asked her two months ago. Besides, seeing his face-splitting victory grin as he reined his horse around to wait for her was worth a zillion times more than the price of dinner.

"So where are you taking us?" he asked, breathing hard.

"Winner's choice." She feigned a look of chagrin. "But please have mercy on my poor, pitiful bank account."

Tripp opted for the restaurant in Fredericksburg where he'd taken her the last time they'd gone out for dinner. After they'd both had a chance to clean up from the ride, Tripp drove into town to pick her up.

His reserved side reemerged over dinner, though—a dinner he barely picked at, she couldn't help noticing. Losing her own appetite, she longed for the lightheartedness they'd shared out on the trail. She'd never admit it aloud, but the strain of trying to stay cheerful and positive for his sake was wearing on her.

He'd grown even more distant by the time he met her at the church the next afternoon to watch the obedience class. Diana finally coaxed out of him that Brooke had phoned early that morning to say his mother had had an especially bad night.

"You should have called me," Diana said, holding his hand as they sat on the park bench.

He glanced away, his mouth hardening. "You worry about me enough as it is."

She wanted to snap at him that two people who truly cared for each other would willingly share their concerns, but the retort froze on the tip of her tongue. Instead, she turned her attention to the class, just in time to see Darby army-crawling out of his "down, stay" position the moment Vince turned his back. In spite of herself, she couldn't hold back a snicker.

Tripp had noticed, too. He squeezed Diana's hand and smiled at her, the corners of his eyes crinkling in a silent plea for forgiveness. "I have a feeling Darby will turn out to be your star therapy pet. Who can resist such cuteness?"

Diana wiggled her brows. "Let's just hope Agnes Kraus agrees."

When the class ended, Diana and Tripp both nodded with satisfaction at the improvement they'd seen in each dog.

"One more class," Sean said as he checked off items on his roster. "So far, I'm expecting all the dogs will pass."

Diana drew air between her teeth. "Even Darby?"

Sean laughed. "Even Darby. He's a work in progress, but he'll get there."

After everyone had left, Diana walked with Tripp to the parking lot. "I promised Aunt Jennie a visit this afternoon. Want to come along?"

"Thanks, but no, not this time." Tripp pressed a hand to his side, and Diana caught a subtle grimace.

"Are you feeling okay? You're not catching something, are you?"

"It's nothing. Probably just too many long days and short nights." His smile seemed forced.

"Well, okay, if you're sure. Go home and get some rest." She stretched up for a quick kiss, then kept her hand on his cheek as she added, "Call me later if you aren't feeling better. I mean it."

His only response was a noncommittal nod.

Knees drawn up on Aunt Jennie's love seat half an hour later, Diana admitted her concerns about counting on a future with Tripp. "Too many times lately, it feels like he's pulling away. Am I being selfish for wanting reassurance?"

"No, sweetie, not at all." Aunt Jennie took a tiny sip of the tea she'd brewed for them. "Just be mindful that with the terrible loss of his mother looming, he'll need time to grieve and heal."

"I'll give him all the time he needs." Diana set aside her empty cup. "The one thing I can't bear," she said with a shudder, "is losing him again."

Aunt Jennie scoffed. "Where's your faith, girl? If God went to all the trouble to send Tripp Willoughby back into your life, do you believe for a minute He won't see this thing through?"

"Of course not." Diana reached across to squeeze her great-aunt's wrinkled hand. "But what if God's plans for this reunion aren't the same as mine? What if He had an entirely different purpose for bringing Tripp to Juniper Bluff?"

"Well, then, it'll be up to the Lord to reveal it." With a wink, Aunt Jennie reached for the teapot.

Diana waved away the offered refill, while her thoughts skipped to a far less romantic reason for Tripp's reappearance in her life. Maybe he was only supposed to help her launch the therapy pets program—something she couldn't confide in Aunt Jennie without spoiling the surprise.

But if that were the case, surely there were a dozen other experienced veterinarians God could have sent Diana's way. Why did it have to be the one man she'd never been able to get out of her heart?

When Tripp's bedside alarm sounded Monday morning, he'd already been up for two hours dealing with a Crohn's flare-up. He limped over to the nightstand and silenced the insistent clamor.

This wasn't looking like a good day to handle squirming puppies and temperamental cats. Reluctantly, Tripp reached for his cell phone.

"Robert, it's Tripp," he began, his whole body tensing as another cramp rolled through him. "Not doing so good this morning. Can you cover my appointments, or should I have Yolanda reschedule?"

His partner agreed to see the morning patients and said he'd take care of rescheduling the afternoon appointments so he could make his farm calls. "You just take it easy and get better, okay?"

Tripp thanked him, then took another dose of his meds and crawled into bed.

Shortly before noon, a call from his sister woke him. Seeing her name on the display, he sat up with a start, ever fearful she'd be calling with bad news. His voice cracked as he answered. "Brooke?"

"Hey, big bro. Sounds like I woke you."

"I, uh...I had to call in sick today. Been napping."

"Oh, no. With all this stress, I bet you haven't been eating right, have you? Remembering your meds?"

"Usually." One hand pressed against the throbbing pain in his abdomen, he was glad his sister couldn't see him just now. "And I'm the big brother, remember? So you can quit bossing me around."

"The big brother who still needs looking after, apparently." Brooke scoffed. "You've let Diana know what you can and can't eat, haven't you?"

Her question only reinforced the doubts he'd been wrestling with. Between his sister giving him the third degree and the cramp twisting through his gut, he was on his last nerve. "I don't need you lecturing me about how I'm handling my stomach issues—or my love life."

"Tripp, I didn't mean—"

"Forget it." Tripp drew a tight breath. "Just tell me how Mom's doing."

"Still declining." Brooke hesitated, her tone growing shaky as she continued. "But her spirits are good. She's amazing, Tripp, shaming us all with her strong faith and how at peace she is about waiting for Jesus to—" Her voice broke.

For a moment, Tripp couldn't find his voice, either. He forced down a painful swallow. "Are we still looking okay for my Thanksgiving trip?"

"For now. The doctors still won't commit to anything definite, and you know Mom's a fighter. Having you here for the holiday is about all she talks about."

Brooke's tentative assurance that their mother could last another month relieved a small measure of Tripp's anxiety. "I've already bought my plane ticket. But if anything changes—"

"I'll call right away."

After saying goodbye, Tripp decided he'd slept long enough and went to the kitchenette to look for something safe to eat. He opened a snack-sized container of applesauce, grabbed a spoon and shuffled out to the porch.

He'd barely sat down when the distant ring of his cell phone sounded from inside the cabin. He almost let it go to voice mail but couldn't take the chance that it wasn't Brooke calling back.

In the bedroom again, he snatched up the phone without checking the display. "Hello?"

"Tripp, are you okay?" Diana. "Doc Ingram just stopped in at the shop and mentioned you called in sick this morning."

"I'll be fine. Probably a…stomach bug…or something." He grimaced at the evasion.

"I'm on my way out there. Could you handle some chicken soup from the deli?"

"Diana, no." Tripp clawed the back of his head. "I'm okay, really."

He could hear each breath she took. "No to the soup," she said slowly, "or no, you don't want me there at all?"

Either answer would get him in deeper trouble than he was already in, so he went with another deflection. "Don't you need to be at the doughnut shop?"

"Kimberly can handle things for the afternoon. Please, Tripp, let me take care of you."

Having Diana "take care of him" through one of these episodes, or something even worse, was the absolute last thing he'd ever wanted. But he sensed turning down her offer now would only raise more questions he wasn't ready to answer. "Okay," he said with a sigh. "Chicken soup might just do the trick."

"Great. I'll be there within the hour."

By the time Diana arrived, Tripp had finished his applesauce and swallowed more cramp meds. The pain had finally subsided. He waited on the porch as she stepped from her car with a white paper sack from the supermarket deli.

She darted up the steps. Standing toe-to-toe with him, she searched his face, then felt his forehead. "You don't feel feverish. How's your stomach?"

"Better." Offering a reassuring smile, he pointed to the bag. "I hope you brought enough for two."

He showed her inside to the kitchenette, where he brought bowls and spoons to the table. While Diana dished out the soup, Tripp filled two glasses with ice water.

As they sat down together, Diana cast him one more look of concern before bowing her head to bless the meal. "And, Lord," she finished, "please knock some sense into this hardheaded man so he doesn't feel like he has to power through troubles on his own."

The first spoonful of soup nearly choked him, but he kept his cool and managed to polish off the entire bowl. It settled well, and Diana's company actually felt nice. Still worn out from the flare-up, though, he soon dozed off in one of the easy chairs. He was vaguely aware of Diana rustling around in the kitchenette, interesting aromas of something on the stove drifting through the cabin.

Sometime later, she jostled his shoulder. "I have to go home and see to my pets, but I found a few things in your fridge—ground turkey, veggies and stuff—and mixed up a casserole. It's warming in the oven whenever you get hungry."

"Thanks," he said, sitting up with a yawn. "Sorry I slept so much."

"You obviously needed the rest." Diana bent down to kiss his forehead, then shook her finger at him. "If you feel worse later, you'd better call."

He only nodded, unwilling to promise. "I'll be fine. Don't worry about me."

"As if." She rolled her eyes and marched to the door.

As it closed behind her, Tripp fought the sudden impulse to go after her and ask her to stay.

Not worry? Tripp had to be kidding. Seemed all she did these days was worry—about being ready for the therapy pets evaluation, about Tripp's mom, and—most of all—whether this romantic revival meant they really could have a future together. Because lately Tripp was giving off all kinds of mixed signals—pulling her in, pushing her away—and Diana was having a terrible time keeping her balance.

Twice after she got home that evening, she almost called Tripp to ask if he was feeling better, then abruptly changed her mind. He'd seemed grateful for her help but also uncomfortable, as if allowing someone else— her?—to take care of him strained some macho part of his psyche.

At least she hoped that's all it was.

By the next morning, she couldn't keep herself from calling. His cell phone went to voice mail, which she took as a sign he was feeling better and made it to work. He returned her call over the noon hour.

"Got your message," he said. "Sorry I couldn't call sooner. We had a full appointment schedule this morning."

Diana pushed aside the salad she'd been eating at her desk. "Are you sure you shouldn't have taken another day to make sure you're over this?"

"I told you, I'm fine." A note of impatience tinged his tone.

"Well, you looked pretty sick yesterday. I was—"

"How many times do I have to tell you, Diana? I *don't* need you worrying about me."

His sharp tone made her flinch. "All right, fine. I have plenty of other things I can be worrying about that don't require dealing with your attitude."

She jammed her thumb on the disconnect button and

slammed the phone facedown on her desk, then dropped her head into her hands.

She'd scarcely moved ten minutes later when Kimberly leaned in the doorway. "Don't tell me—lovers' quarrel?"

Massaging her temple, Diana released an exasperated sigh. "Can we rewind the calendar to last summer? Life sure seemed a lot simpler then."

"Simpler. But a lot less interesting."

"I can do boring. Boring is nice. Boring is—"

Diana's part-time counter girl, Nora, tapped on the door frame. "Hey, Diana, somebody's asking for you out front."

"A customer?"

Nora smirked. "Your boyfriend."

"Tripp?" Diana's stomach plummeted. "Tripp's *here?*"

Kimberly cast her an enigmatic smile. "Guess you'd better go see what he wants."

Nora and Kimberly both slipped out, while Diana squeezed her eyes shut and prayed for calm. Then, head held high, she marched from the office.

Tripp paced on the other side of the counter. Seeing her, he halted, his eyes pleading. "Di. Please don't be mad."

"Don't I have a right to be?" Sniffing back a surge of emotion, she scanned the shop. Good, no other customers at the moment. She pressed her fingertips into the countertop. "Tripp, what's going on with us? You have me so confused I can hardly think straight."

"Not my intention. I'm just…" He pulled a hand down his face, his gaze sweeping up, down and sideways as if searching for words.

Too tired to argue, Diana decided to make it simpler for him. "Just slowing things down for a while. I get it."

He winced. "It's not the same, not like before."

"That's what I'm counting on." She took his hand and squeezed hard. "If you need slow, we'll go slow. I'm not going anywhere."

Diana didn't hear from Tripp for the rest of the week, and it took every bit of willpower not to call or stop by the clinic. She began to wonder if he'd even put in an appearance at the final obedience class on Sunday. But if he needed space, what choice did she have but to give it to him?

When her parents invited her to go to lunch with them after church, she begged off. Instead, she spent the first part of the afternoon reviewing her therapy pet notes and making sure she was still on track with the paperwork.

As she'd feared, Tripp didn't make it to the class. And neither did one of the students. A few minutes after Sean got started, Diana's cell phone rang.

"Sorry for not letting you know sooner," the woman said, "but my daughter's work schedule got changed unexpectedly and I need to watch my grandson. Afraid I can't make it to the class."

"That's okay," Diana said. "I'll ask Sean if he can offer a makeup session."

"No, don't bother. It looks like I'll be keeping my grandson fairly regularly from now on, so you'd better not count on me as a volunteer."

"Oh, I see." Covering her disappointment, Diana expressed her understanding and invited the woman to get in touch if her situation changed.

Great. Agnes Kraus's final evaluation and therapy pet volunteer training was only a week away. If Diana lost one more volunteer, she'd be below the minimum necessary to get her therapy pets chapter approved.

Back home again, she pored over the original list of possible volunteers and zeroed in on those whose dogs already had obedience training. Could any who'd initially declined be convinced to reconsider? Maybe Tripp would help—

Diana bit her lip. No, she was on her own for now.

At the rate things were going, she might *always* be on her own.

It sure felt like it when she and Tripp hardly spoke at all over the next week. They shared brief phone calls, but their conversations mainly touched on how his mother was doing and if Diana was ready for Agnes Kraus's visit on Saturday.

"I'd really like you to be there," Diana said when Tripp called her Friday evening.

"I'll try," was all he said. "But either way, you'll do great."

At the doughnut shop on Saturday, Diana spilled more coffee in a single morning than she usually did in an entire year. She shouldn't be so nervous—she still had a full contingent of volunteers, all eight with obedience certification and the required veterinary forms. But Agnes Kraus would be judging by her own set of criteria. Whether Diana's loyal band of dog owners could pass the strict criteria to form a Visiting Pet Pals chapter, she wouldn't venture a guess.

As she mopped up yet another spill on the service counter, Kimberly came in from the kitchen with a tray of muffins. "For pity's sake, Diana, go do some book-keeping or something. Let Ethan take over the register."

"He's busy busing tables. Anyway, I'd rather spill coffee than risk transposing numbers in the accounts." Pushing out her lower lip to blow a strand of hair from her eyes, Diana gave her attention to the next customer.

Over her lunch break, she reviewed her checklist one more time to make sure she hadn't overlooked anything. Shortly after three, Kimberly shooed her out the door with strict instructions to call later and tell her how it went.

She'd arranged for the volunteers to gather once again on the lawn behind the church. By 3:25, seven of the eight dog owners had shown up. A few minutes later, a dark blue SUV pulled into the parking lot, and a tall, red-haired woman in a tailored blouse and dressy slacks stepped out. With the added effect of the woman's dignified bun and square-shaped tortoiseshell glasses, Diana felt like she was back in high school and about to be disciplined by the principal for too many tardies.

Wiping sweaty palms on her jeans, and suddenly feeling completely underdressed, Diana strode over and introduced herself. "So nice to finally meet you in person, Mrs. Kraus. Did you have any trouble finding us?"

"Not at all." Head tilted, the woman surveyed the group now walking their dogs around the lawn and chatting with each other. "Only seven?"

"The last one should be here any minute." *I hope!* The only person missing was Kelly Nesbit with her terrier mix, Freckles. Kelly rarely arrived late for anything, and Diana was growing concerned. "Do you want to wait, or should we get started? I have the signed agreement from the assisted-living center, along with all the dogs' health records and temperament assessments, if you want to look at those first."

When Mrs. Kraus agreed, Diana led her over to the bench where she'd left her tote. While the woman perused the paperwork, Diana kept an eye on the parking lot. Shortly, her cell phone buzzed with a text from Kelly: Emergency at the walk-in clinic. Can't get away. So sorry!

Drawing a bolstering breath, Diana informed Mrs. Kraus. "But I know Kelly really wants to participate, and her dog went through obedience training last year." She riffled through the file folder. "See? Here's the copy of his certificate, plus all the veterinary forms."

"I'm sorry, but I can't approve a dog and handler without personally observing them." Rising, the woman returned the forms she'd just been reviewing. "Unfortunately, without eight qualified volunteers and dogs, your group doesn't meet the qualifications for a Visiting Pet Pals chapter."

Diana rose and stood in front of Mrs. Kraus. "But you've come all this way. Surely you won't turn us down because we're short one person?"

"We have strict guidelines. If I were to make an exception for you—"

"But you just said they were guidelines. People make exceptions to guidelines all the time."

"I can't, not without approval from our board of directors." With an apologetic smile, Mrs. Kraus withdrew her key fob from her handbag. "Contact me again after the first of the year. I'll be happy to reschedule."

So much for Aunt Jennie's birthday surprise. Diana had already arranged with the director at the center to hold their first pet visit a week from next Monday. She'd reserved the community room and had been working on plans all week to make it a fun celebration for Aunt Jennie and all the residents.

"No," Diana said, hoping she sounded more authoritative than whiny. "No, it *has* to be today. You can't—"

Someone's firm but gentle grip settled on her shoulder, and the next voice she heard was Tripp's.

"Hello, Mrs. Kraus. I'm Dr. Willoughby, and these dogs are my patients." He stepped up beside Diana. "Surely we can work something out. Diana's invested too much time, energy and heart in this project to have it fall through on such a minor technicality."

The pressure of Tripp's hand brought the welcome reassurance Diana needed. Now she could only hold her breath and hope their combined pleas would change Mrs. Kraus's mind.

"As I was telling Ms. Matthews," the woman said, "I don't have authorization to make such a decision."

Tripp glanced at Diana. "Who are we missing?"

"Kelly and Freckles," she murmured. "Kelly got caught at the clinic."

With a thoughtful nod, Tripp addressed Mrs. Kraus. "Then how about this? Go ahead and evaluate these dogs and owners now. If the last volunteer doesn't make it before you're ready to begin the volunteer training session, I will personally arrange to get her and her dog to your location sometime within the next few days."

Indecision played across the woman's face. "Well, I suppose that's an option. Nothing says the evaluation and training can't be done elsewhere, or that all dogs have to be seen on the same day."

"So," Diana said, confidence returning, "once all

the dogs and owners are approved, you can certify our group as a chapter, right? And we can start our visitations."

"Correct." Mrs. Kraus retrieved a clipboard from her satchel. "Very well, then. Shall we get started?"

As the woman strode over to where the owners mingled with their dogs, Diana released her pent-up breath. She swiveled to face Tripp. "Thank you. I didn't think you were coming."

"Nothing could keep me from being here today. I—" He wavered, his gaze shifting toward the bench. "Can we continue this discussion sitting down?"

Noticing his pallor, Diana tugged him over to the bench. "Are you okay?"

His gaze slid sideways as he mumbled, "Still having some stomach problems. It's nothing."

"It's the stress of everything, isn't it? Have you been to see a doctor?"

"It's under control." Tripp reached for Diana's hand. "Can we talk about something else?"

He was closing himself off again. Diana yanked her hand away and folded her arms. "So you're feeling sick and yet still found the strength to swoop in here like Superman to save my therapy pets program. And now you won't talk about it? What does that say about our relationship?"

Tripp's gaze locked with hers. "It says I care."

He had her there. Lips pursed, she glanced away. As much as she'd like to pursue this discussion, today wasn't the ideal time, not with so much riding on today. She released a huff and pushed up from the bench. "This isn't over, Tripp. One of these days, maybe you'll finally be ready to share all of yourself, not just the parts you think I can handle."

She lifted her hands in an exasperated gesture, then with a brisk shake of her head she marched across the lawn.

Chapter Ten

Once all the dogs had passed Agnes Kraus's evaluation, Tripp decided not to stick around to watch the training session. He wasn't feeling that great anyway—and he hadn't been lying when he went along with Diana's suggestion that it was stress. Between agonizing over the thought of losing his mother and doing his best not to permanently wreck things with Diana, his life couldn't get much more stressful.

He skipped church Sunday morning in an attempt to nip his latest flare-up in the bud so he wouldn't have to take any more time off from work. On Monday he followed through on his promise to Diana and contacted Kelly Nesbit to see if she'd be willing to take Freckles to San Antonio to meet with Agnes Kraus. Kelly had a day off on Thursday and said she'd be happy to make the drive, so Tripp phoned Mrs. Kraus to set up the appointment.

On Thursday evening, Diana called. "I thought you'd want to know, Kelly and Freckles passed with flying colors and my chapter's been approved."

"Never had any doubts. Congratulations."

"We're holding a practice session on Saturday to get ready for our first visit to the assisted-living center. Any chance you can come?"

The hopeful lilt in her tone tugged at Tripp's heart. He pushed aside his half-eaten plate of scrambled eggs. "I'll see how things go this weekend." Hoping to distract her from any health-related questions, he changed the subject. "Found a home for another kitten today. Just one left now, plus mama cat."

"Really? I'm so glad. I'm still working on Pastor Terry's wife. She's hinted a few times she'd love to have a kitten." Diana sighed. "I don't know what to do about the mama. Nobody seems interested in a full-grown cat. They just don't have the cute factor kittens do."

Tripp shifted and stretched out one leg. "I had an idea about mama cat. She's made herself right at home at the clinic. What if we adopted her as the clinic cat?"

"You could do that? Oh, Tripp, I love the idea!"

He smiled to himself, glad he could bring a little more happiness into Diana's life. "We'll probably change her name, though. Yolanda's been calling her 'Sandy.'"

"A perfect name."

A brief but pleasant silence settled between them. Then Tripp asked, "How are the party plans coming?"

"Everything's set for Monday evening at the assisted-living center. I can't wait."

"Hope I can come by, at least for a bit."

"Me, too. I know your California flight leaves pretty early the next morning." A pause. "Tripp? Take care of yourself, will you?"

"Yeah. Thanks." He pressed his lips together. "I'll

do my best to be there for your practice session this weekend."

On Saturday, though, Tripp got drafted by Robert to assist with emergency surgery on a horse with an impacted tooth that had become infected. They wrapped things up too late for Tripp to make it to the practice session, and by then he barely had enough reserves left to clean up and fall into bed.

By Monday morning, a November cold front had blown in, bringing gusty winds and intermittent rain showers. The miserable weather seemed apt for Tripp's gloomy state of mind, a perfect day to bury himself in work.

As he entered the clinic through the back door, he caught Yolanda's voice as she spoke with a client.

"I'm sorry, Vince, but Doc Willoughby seems to be running a little late this morning," she said. "He's been fighting a stomach bug off and on for the past couple of weeks."

"But I've got to get Darby fixed up quick." Vince's tone sounded urgent. "We're doing our first Visiting Pet Pals event tonight."

"Let me try to reach Doc Willoughby. Can you—"

Tripp stepped into the area behind the reception counter. "What's going on with Darby?"

Yolanda whirled around. "I thought you might be under the weather again."

"I'm okay." Giving Yolanda's shoulder a pat, he peered over the counter for a look at Vince's mutt. "What happened, fella?"

Seated on his haunches, Darby whined softly and held up his left forepaw.

"I let him out to take care of business after breakfast, and he decided to chase a squirrel," Vince explained. "The grass was slippery from the rain, and he tripped on a tree root. Been limping ever since."

"Let's take a look. Bring him on back."

In the exam room, Tripp pulled a rolling stool over and sat down to perform his examination. He palpated Darby's leg from shoulder to paw, then gently flexed the joints to determine which movements caused discomfort.

"Nothing appears to be broken," he said, straightening. "Most likely a simple sprain. The best thing for Darby is rest and an ice pack."

Stroking the big dog's head, Vince heaved a sigh. "Then we shouldn't join the rest of the group at the center this evening?"

Tripp gnawed the inside of his lip. He hated disappointing Vince, but even more, he knew how much a full contingent of volunteers tonight would mean to Diana. "See how he's doing later this afternoon. If the swelling has gone down and he isn't favoring the leg so much, it would probably be safe to take him over for at least part of the evening."

"Well, you'll be there, right, in case we have any problems?"

"Uh, not sure I can make it."

Vince's mouth fell open. "What? After all you did to help Diana make this happen? Come on, Doc, you gotta be there."

Tripp sat forward, elbows on his knees. "The thing is, I'm leaving in the morning to spend Thanksgiving with my family, and—" He clamped his teeth together against the heartbreaking ache in his chest. "It could be the last time I see my mom."

"Aw, Doc, I'm real sorry. We all understand you've got a lot on your mind."

"Which is why I'm not sure my being there tonight is a good idea. I'd just put a damper on everyone's enjoyment—especially Diana's."

"That's just plumb crazy. You mean the world to her. Should have heard how she talked about you last weekend at our volunteer meeting."

Tripp swallowed. "What exactly did she say?"

"Mostly what a hard time you were having with your mom being sick and how we might still be waiting on approval if you hadn't stepped in with Mrs. Kraus." Vince quirked his mouth in a dubious frown. "So you better not let her down, Doc. Or the rest of us, either, because we're all counting on you."

Warmth spread through Tripp's insides. "I'll think about it," he promised. "Maybe I'll see you at the party, after all."

Prickles of excitement darted up and down Diana's spine as she tapped on Aunt Jennie's door. When her great-aunt invited her in, she swept the little woman into a hug. "Happy birthday!"

Aunt Jennie released a hearty chuckle. "Got plenty to be happy about. Making it to ninety-three is nothing to sneeze at!"

"Mom and Dad are meeting us in the dining room. Ready to go over?"

"Just let me get my sweater. It's always so chilly in there." Snatching a baby blue cardigan off a chair, Aunt Jennie took Diana's arm. "So glad you and your folks could come over and have dinner with me. Makes my birthday extra special."

Diana could hardly wait to make her great-aunt's day even more special.

In the dining room, her parents met them at a festively decorated table for four. As Diana's dad seated her, Aunt Jennie gasped with delight. Her smile stretched even wider when the server brought out plates heaping with some of her favorite foods: sugar-cured ham, marshmallow-topped sweet potatoes, baked apples, creamed peas and yeasty dinner rolls.

"Don't forget to save room for ice cream and cake," Diana said with a wink.

Laughing, Aunt Jennie squeezed Diana's hand. "Oh, my, you're spoiling me."

Taking a quick peek at her watch, Diana replied with a tight-lipped smile. Her volunteers should be checking in at the front desk anytime now. They'd be ready to make their entrance shortly after Aunt Jennie and the other residents finished dinner and gathered in the community room.

Halfway through dinner, Aunt Jennie remarked, "How is your sweet young man doing, honey? You haven't brought him to see me in a while."

Releasing a tremulous breath, Diana clutched the napkin in her lap. "He's been busy. And still very worried about his mother."

"Oh, yes. Please let him know I'm keeping him in my prayers—" Aunt Jennie's eyes narrowed as she looked toward the opposite door. "Could be mistaken, but I think I just saw him peek in."

Heart hammering, Diana twisted to look but caught only a glimpse of a plaid shirtsleeve before whoever it was disappeared around the corner. She'd hoped Tripp would try to be there, but she hadn't dared to count on it.

Excusing herself, she rose on shaky legs. She found him in the community room mingling with the therapy pet volunteers. Tripp glanced up from his conversation with Kelly Nesbit, his gaze locking with Diana's. He said something to Kelly, then ambled over. His mouth twitched in a nervous smile. "Looks like everything's going according to plan."

"So far. Aunt Jennie's going to be so surprised." Diana studied him. "How are you feeling?"

"Better." He shoved his hands into the pockets of slim black jeans. "Couldn't bear to miss your great-aunt's expression when she's greeted by all these furry friends."

"I can't wait, either." Diana glanced up with a sincere smile. "You helped make this happen, and I haven't begun to thank you enough."

"No need. I've enjoyed every minute of it." He looked past Diana, a flicker of uncertainty in his expression. "Mr. Matthews. Nice to see you again."

"Hello, Tripp." Diana's father rested a protective arm around her shoulder. "Sweetie, they're ready to bring out Aunt Jennie's birthday cake."

"Be right there, Dad." She waited for her father to step away, then murmured, "I should make sure my volunteers are all set."

"Right. If there's anything I can do, just ask."

She replied with a quick nod, then shared some last-minute instructions for the volunteers before rejoining her family in the dining room. Her mother signaled the server to bring the cake to the table, and Aunt Jennie's eyes sparkled brighter than the twinkling candles atop

the German chocolate cake. As they began the birthday song, the other residents took notice and chimed in.

As the applause died down, Diana took the opportunity to make her announcement. "Don't forget, the
party continues in the community room right after dinner. Please join us!"

"There's *more*?" Aunt Jennie asked.

"Oh, yes." Diana grinned. "The fun is just beginning."

Finding a chair in an out-of-the-way corner of the
community room, Tripp settled in to watch as residents
began to gather after dinner. Those first glimpses of
eight mannerly pooches of all shapes, colors and sizes
brought varied reactions—everything from bewilderment, to curious smiles, to full-out grins and laughter.

Tripp couldn't help smiling, himself. This was even
better than when he'd worked with a therapy pets group
while doing his veterinary internship. Not that tonight's
experience was so different, but because he was getting
to share it with Diana.

He looked toward the entrance to see her escorting
her great-aunt into the room. The tiny, white-haired
woman's eyes grew big as saucers. She threw a hand
to her mouth to cover a gasp.

"Oh, my, look at all the puppies!" Laughing, Jennie clutched Diana's wrist. "How delightful! Can we
pet them?"

"That's why they're here." Beaming, Diana showed
her great-aunt to a chair near the center of the room.
"This is your birthday surprise, Aunt Jennie."

One by one, Diana had the volunteers come over
and introduce their dogs. Jennie oohed and aahed over

each of them, caressing their heads and tickling them under their chins. After she'd had a few minutes to enjoy the dogs, the volunteers began taking their pets around to meet other residents. Some responded shyly, others eagerly, but Tripp could see in each face the pure joy of giving and receiving this singular gift of affection.

While he watched from his corner, Vince and Janice Mussell wandered over with Darby. "You're awful quiet over here," Vince remarked.

"Just taking it all in." Tripp gave Darby a pat while unobtrusively checking the dog's leg. "Looks like this fella's doing better this evening."

"Followed your orders with the cold packs and kept him off his feet most of the afternoon. He was rarin' to go by suppertime."

"Isn't this the most fun ever?" Janice's gaze swept the room. "And so rewarding. Diana says we're going to try scheduling visits twice a month."

A stooped gentleman hobbled over, leaning on his cane. "Can I pet this boy again? Reminds me an awful lot of Duke, my boyhood dog. Never stopped missing that sweet old guy."

Vince and Janice sat down with the elderly man, and while he showered Darby with attention and reminisced about Duke, Tripp decided it was time to slip out.

He made it as far as the foyer when Diana caught up with him. "You're not leaving already, are you?"

"I've got that flight to catch in the morning, remember?"

"Oh, Tripp, I wish I could go with you."

"You have your shop to run. Besides, you should be with your own family for the holiday."

Diana dropped her forehead against his chest. He

was right, she couldn't exactly skip out on her mother's Thanksgiving feast. They'd have Aunt Jennie with them this year, too. "You'll keep in touch, though?"

"I promise."

She sniffed loudly and raked her hand across her cheeks. "If your mom—I mean, when the time comes—"

"I'll let you know." He pulled her close, his throat closing over the words he had to say before he left. "Don't ever forget how much I love you, Di. Always have, always will."

"Tripp—"

"Walk me to my car. I need to get on the road to San Antonio."

Her steps faltered as he guided her toward the exit. "Now?"

"My flight leaves at six a.m. I booked a room for tonight at a hotel near the airport."

He was back to all business again. And not fooling her for a moment. They stopped beside his SUV. "Tripp?"

"Yeah?" He climbed in behind the wheel.

"I'm still in love with you, too."

Chapter Eleven

Watching Tripp drive away, Diana felt her heart ripping in two. She'd have given anything to be with him during what could turn out to be the most difficult Thanksgiving anyone could face. Instead, all she could do was pray for him.

For the present, though, she took comfort in knowing she'd made her beloved great-aunt's birthday special. When Diana telephoned Aunt Jennie the next day during a break at the shop, the sweet woman spent almost the entire conversation raving about the party and the time spent with all the adorable, well-behaved dogs. According to Aunt Jennie, everyone else at the center had fallen in love with the dogs, too, and couldn't wait for their return.

"I'm scheduling another visit in a couple of weeks," Diana assured her. "In the meantime, I've gotten the okay to bring Alice, my rabbit, for an afternoon visit next Sunday. She's not as playful as the dogs, but she's great for cuddling."

Changing topics, Diana reminded Aunt Jennie

she'd be picking her up on Thursday morning to spend Thanksgiving with Diana's parents.

"I can't wait. Much as I've enjoyed the meals they serve us here, I'm ready for your dad's famous smoked turkey and your mother's delicious corn bread dressing."

On Thanksgiving morning, Aunt Jennie already had her coat on and was waiting for Diana in the lobby. The day held just enough nip in the air that Diana hoped her parents had a cozy fire going in the wood-burning stove. They did, and Diana settled Aunt Jennie in a padded rocker close by, then brought her a steaming cup of tea with honey and lemon.

"Dad's out back keeping an eye on the smoker." Diana tuned the TV to a holiday parade broadcast for her great-aunt to watch. "Need anything else before I help Mom in the kitchen?"

"I'll be just fine, sweetie." Aunt Jennie patted Diana's hand and looked up with a concerned smile. "Any word from your young man today?"

Glancing out the broad picture window at the barren pastures, Diana sucked in a tiny breath. "No, not yet."

"You should call him, let him know you're thinking about him."

"Maybe later. I don't want to intrude on his family time." Diana gave her great-aunt a quick kiss on the forehead, then excused herself to help her mother with dinner preparations.

It didn't take Mom long to notice Diana's preoccupation, especially after she accidentally dropped one of her mother's crystal water glasses on the tile floor.

"It's okay, honey," Mom said, swooping in with a broom and dustpan. "It's just a glass."

"I know, but—" Making a growling noise in her

throat, Diana tore off a handful of paper towels and wet them at the sink, then knelt to help her mother clean up the remaining glass fragments.

When they finished, Mom pulled Diana close for a hug. "This is all about Tripp, isn't it?"

"I hate being so conflicted." Diana pressed her temple against her mother's. "Right before he drove away Monday night, I finally told him I'm still in love with him."

Chuckling, Mom shifted to face Diana. "And that has you conflicted?"

"Actually, more like terrified. Because I can't shake the sense that something's going to happen to keep us apart."

I'm still in love with you, too.

Every time Diana's words whispered through Tripp's mind, he thought his heart would burst right out of his chest. The memory had carried him all the way to San Antonio, comforted him through a restless night at the airport hotel and buoyed his flagging hopes during the long flight to Los Angeles.

The next two days and nights spent at his mother's bedside, though, blurred such hopes into oblivion. Mom had grown so weak and pale, she was a shadow of the woman he remembered from the last time he'd visited. She seemed to sleep most of the time, and whether she heard the conversations going on around her, Tripp couldn't tell. He could only thank God he'd made it in time to spend this last Thanksgiving with her.

As he sat holding his mother's hand on Thursday morning, Brooke asked him for some help in the kitchen. Reluctant to leave his mother's side, he rose and brushed the papery-thin skin of her forehead with a kiss. His dad immediately took his place beside Mom's bed, and the tragically endearing expression on Dad's face as he gazed at his sleeping wife just about did Tripp in.

Halting outside the kitchen door, he squeezed his eyes shut as a vision of Diana someday wearing that same expression at his bedside smacked him hard.

I'm still in love with you, too.

His belly cramped. He didn't realize his groan was audible until Brooke called his name.

She jabbed her finger toward a chair at the dinette. "Get in here and sit down. And don't pretend with me that you're not hurting. It's written all over your face."

One hand pressed against the pain in his abdomen, he glared at his sister. "Drop it, will you? I don't need—"

Their father's anguished cry rang out from the other room, and they both rushed to Mom's bedside. The hospice nurse stood on the opposite side, her stethoscope pressed to Mom's chest. Moments later, she silently shook her head.

That quickly, it was over. Within the hour, two gentlemen in dark suits arrived from the mortuary and took Tripp's mother away.

Sick with grief, worsened by his unrelenting remorse over not being able to save Mom with one of his own kidneys, Tripp collapsed on his bed and stayed there for the rest of the day.

Dusk was falling when Brooke peeked in on him. "Hey, brother mine. Come eat something. We've still got all this Thanksgiving food in the oven." She sighed. "And we all need to keep our strength up for what happens next."

With a barely suppressed moan, Tripp eased his legs

off the side of the bed and sat up. "Not hungry, but I'll try."

"Good." Brooke tucked an arm around his shoulder. "Oh, and I left messages for Diana about the funeral. I know you don't feel like talking yet, but you should call her. She'll be anxious to hear from you."

Nodding, Tripp made a vague promise to call Diana soon. The problem was, he had no idea what he'd say to her. The last thing he wanted was to break her heart again, but these last few days had reaffirmed his convictions that he had to spare her even the remotest possibility of suffering through what his dad had just endured. But if he suddenly told her there was no chance of a future together, she'd beg for explanations and, once again, he'd hold back, because Diana was just stubborn enough to stay with him no matter what.

And the thought of seeing her again at Mom's funeral? He hated himself for thinking this, but a part of him hoped Diana would be too busy to come.

Diana had barely walked in the door at home after dropping off Aunt Jennie at her apartment when her cell phone rang. The display showed an out-of-area phone number but no name, so it couldn't be Tripp. Probably another of those annoying robocalls. With her suddenly starving cats yowling at her feet, she let the call go to voice mail.

Later, after all the pets were taken care of and she'd warmed some leftovers for her own supper, she listened to the message. When she heard Brooke Willoughby's voice, her heart plummeted to her toes.

"Hello, Diana. It's been a long, long time, huh?" Brooke sounded as if she'd been crying. "I'm calling for Tripp because he's…well, he's taking this pretty hard. But he said you'd want to know when Mom passed away—the funeral arrangements and such."

With a sniffle, Brooke reported that their mother had slipped away peacefully in her sleep around eleven that morning. A quick time-difference calculation told Diana she would have been helping her mother sweep up the broken crystal around that time.

"We're taking Mom home to Austin for the burial," Brooke's message continued shakily. "Services will be next Monday. Soon as I hang up, I'll text you the details." A pause. "I'm sure you're worried about Tripp. He's just…he's going to need some time. And I really hope you can come to the funeral, because we'd all love to see you again."

The voice mail ended, and Diana switched over to view the text. Tears rolled down her cheeks as she read the name and address of the church she used to attend with the Willoughby family whenever she visited Tripp back in college. Those had been such happy times, sharing smiles while they sang the worship songs, holding hands as they bowed their heads for prayer. And Peggy Willoughby always planned the most fun Sunday afternoons. She'd have the whole family pitching in to put homemade pizzas together for lunch, or the girls would chat as they chopped salad veggies while the guys went out to the patio to grill steaks. Afterward, sometimes they'd walk to a nearby park and play disc golf, or if it was cold or rainy, they'd gather round the dining room table and play board games until Diana, Brooke and Tripp had to pack up for the drive back to campus.

The memories kept coming, until Diana had soaked several tissues and decided it was time to get practical.

First, she called Kimberly and asked her to cover the shop for a couple of days. "I'll drive over to Austin on Sunday afternoon and probably return sometime Tuesday. Will that work for you?"

"Absolutely. No worries, hon. Got someone lined up to take care of your animals?"

"My teenage neighbor knows the routine. I'm calling her next." Diana thanked Kimberly and said she'd see her in the morning. A few minutes later, she'd made arrangements for the pets and also reserved a room at the hotel Brooke had mentioned in her text.

Now all she had to do was survive the next few days until she could see Tripp again.

After the Sunday worship service and a quick bite of lunch with her parents, Diana climbed in her car and headed for Austin. The drive took just over two hours, and by four o'clock, she had checked in to her hotel room and hung her dark navy dress in the closet so the travel wrinkles would hang out.

Sitting on the bed, she stared at her cell phone and pondered giving Tripp a call to let him know she was in town. He'd texted yesterday afternoon, a curt message informing her they were in Austin and staying with church friends.

She'd texted back, Glad you made it safely. See you soon. Praying.

No reply.

She had to assume they were all exhausted beyond imagining, and with burial arrangements still to be finalized, Tripp had plenty on his mind without engaging in chitchat. Tomorrow would come soon enough, and Diana could finally surround him with the love she'd been storing up since he left after Aunt Jennie's party last Monday night.

For the past twelve years, if she were honest. The bitterness she'd clung to in the beginning, then the couldn't-care-less pretense that came later, had only masked her true feelings. No matter how staunchly she'd claimed to be over Tripp Willoughby, having him back in her life these past several weeks had proved her wrong. Utterly and completely wrong.

The next morning, after a few bites of the hotel's complimentary breakfast along with three cups of strong coffee to counteract a virtually sleepless night, Diana dressed for the funeral. She left shortly after nine thirty for the ten o'clock service. The route was so familiar, but there had been a few changes since the last time she'd traveled these streets—a new strip shopping mall, more fast-food restaurants, a business plaza. Across the road from the church, a modern, up-scale apartment complex filled what used to be a vacant lot. The church itself had grown, too, a breezeway now connecting the sanctuary to a two-story educational building and gymnasium.

Time hadn't stopped. Not for the community, not for this church, not for Diana and Tripp. Their feelings for each other had grown and changed, as well. The bud-ding romance of their college years, though unexpect-edly cut short, now held the promise of growing into something much deeper and more mature. More lasting, too, Diana prayed. It made her heart flutter to imagine what came next.

Stepping from her car, she strode across the rapidly filling parking lot and joined other mourners on their way into the sanctuary. An usher handed her a memorial bulletin and invited her to sign the guest book. She waited her turn at the stand by the inner doors, then found a seat about halfway to the front.

Sorrow billowed in her chest at the sight of the closed coffin and floral arrangements in front of the altar. Peggy Willoughby's portrait sat on an easel nearby— soft, brown curls sprinkled with gray framing smiling eyes so much like Tripp's, it made Diana's heart clench.

A few minutes before ten, a side door opened to the left of the chancel. The pastor emerged—someone new since Diana had been here last—followed by Brooke and Tripp, their father supported between them. The poor man, thinner and more stooped than Diana recalled, had a dazed look about him. Brooke had changed little. Even her red-rimmed eyes didn't betray her innate self-assurance, evident in the set of her chin and purposeful steps.

But Tripp—oh, Tripp! Taking in his haggard appearance, Diana nearly started from the pew. Hollow cheeks, dark circles under his eyes and the grim set to his mouth testified to the agony of grief he'd endured these past several days. She wished he'd look her way so that she could silently convey her love and support, but he barely glanced up before taking the front pew with his father and sister.

The service began, and Diana could hardly tear her gaze from the back of Tripp's head. Though his father wept openly and Brooke dried her eyes several times, Tripp sat stoically, even when Brooke strode to the lectern to say a few words about their mother.

Following the concluding prayers, the pastor invited family and friends to proceed to the cemetery for the graveside service, after which the Willoughbys would receive guests at a luncheon in the fellowship hall. Diana filed out to her car with the others. The cemetery was only a few blocks away, and soon she stood weeping silently on the periphery as the pastor read the Twenty-third Psalm and commended Peggy to her heavenly Father.

Still, Tripp didn't seem aware of her presence, and before she could approach him, the funeral director whisked him and his father and sister into a limousine for the return to the church. There, at least, Diana hoped to finally have a few minutes to hold and comfort him.

Arriving back at the church parking lot, she followed the other mourners to a large, first-floor room in the new building addition. Tripp and his family stood inside the main doors to receive greetings and accept condolences, and with each step that brought her nearer, Diana's pulse notched up.

At last, she stood in front of Brooke. Her former roommate gasped in happy surprise and wrapped her in a warm hug. "Diana! I'm so glad you came."

"Me, too." Diana's voice cracked. "I'm so, so sorry about your mom."

Breaking away, Brooke looped her arm through her father's. "Dad, here's Diana."

Mr. Willoughby's smile broadened. "How are you, honey? Gracious, you look just the same. I wish—" Tearing up again, he pulled her close for a kiss on the cheek, then whispered, "It made Peggy so happy to know you and Tripp found each other again."

Unable to speak, Diana merely nodded as Mr. Willoughby handed her off to Tripp. Holding both his hands, she felt suddenly shy as she looked up at him. His lips trembled in the beginnings of a smile that quickly faded. She moved closer to draw him into a comforting embrace but sensed him stiffen before he edged away.

"I, uh…we can talk later," he murmured, nodding toward the line behind her. "Sorry."

"Of course." Diana stepped away. She had no right to feel snubbed, but she couldn't help it. It felt as if Tripp had just slammed a door in her face.

Brooke reached past her father and Tripp to catch Diana's arm. "We have a reserved table at the far end. Sit with us, okay?"

"Are you sure?" Diana glanced at Tripp, hoping for his agreement, but he'd turned away to speak with someone else.

"Absolutely," Brooke said, then added with a meaningful smile, "You're practically family."

Brooke's reassurance restored a measure of Diana's confidence. Tripp's detachment had to be grief related. It must have been torture knowing nothing could be done to help his mother, then to witness her rapid decline, to be with her as she breathed her last… Diana couldn't imagine losing one of her own parents, or even Aunt Jennie, to a lengthy and devastating illness.

With a sobering breath, she crossed to the buffet table. As she filled a plate, a few of the Willoughbys' old friends recognized her from years gone by and welcomed her back. Their kind words warmed her, especially when they spoke to her as if she, too, had suffered a loss. She truly felt as if she had, because if things did work out between her and Tripp, she'd never get to experience knowing Peggy not just as her boyfriend's mother but as her cherished mother-in-law.

By the time the receiving line had dwindled and the Willoughbys could get some lunch, Diana had almost finished. Arriving at the table, Tripp faltered as if surprised to see Diana there. With a hesitant smile, he took the chair at her left, and she noticed his plate held little more than a slice of ham and a small serving of green beans. Before she could comment, though, Brooke and her father sat down on Diana's other side.

"I'm worn out." Brooke released a muted groan and took a sip of iced tea.

Diana touched Brooke's arm. "Thanks again for inviting me to sit with you. It's an honor I wasn't expecting."

"Wouldn't have it any other way." With a wink, Brooke added, "And don't tell anyone, but I'm kicking my shoes off under the table."

"My lips are sealed."

Tripp and his father both ate in silence—or rather, mostly picked at their food—while Brooke asked Diana all kinds of questions about what she'd been doing since college. Diana couldn't tell whether her old friend's chatter was genuine interest or just her way of dealing with grief. Recalling what she knew of Brooke from their college days, probably both.

A sudden motion to her left made her glance at Tripp. A grimace marred his features. Short, moaning breaths slipped between his dry lips as he leaned forward and clutched his abdomen.

Diana swiveled to face him. "Tripp, what is it?"

Eyes squeezed shut, he shook his head. His face had gone deathly pale, and the moans had become one long, keening cry.

Panicking, Diana whirled around to get Brooke's

attention, but she'd already shoved her chair back and was hurrying around to Tripp's side.

"Hospital," Tripp gasped. "Now."

Chapter Twelve

Before Diana realized what was happening, several people had rushed to help. She scooted out of the way as someone Brooke addressed as Dr. Halvorson stepped in. By then, Tripp was doubled over in obvious pain and verging on unconsciousness.

After a brief debate about whether to call for an ambulance, the doctor recommended driving Tripp directly to the emergency room. Two other men came over and, looping Tripp's arms over their shoulders, walked him out to Brooke's rental car, parked just outside.

Terrified, Diana hurried after them. She caught Brooke as she climbed in behind the steering wheel. "Where are you taking him? I want to come."

Brooke named the hospital. "It's not far. Meet us there."

By the time Diana got to her own car and brought up the hospital location on her map app, the Willoughbys were a good five minutes ahead. Then she had to deal with traffic and got stuck in the right lane when she needed to make a left turn. When she finally found her way to the parking area outside the emergency room, she was ready to claw through the windshield.

She raced through the double doors and surveyed the busy waiting area. No sign of Brooke, her father or Tripp—and she knew this was the right hospital because she recognized Brooke's car parked at the drop-off curb.

Her worries skyrocketed. Nobody got seen this quickly in the ER unless it was a life-or-death situation. *Dear Lord, please. I can't lose him now!*

Fighting down panic, she approached the check-in desk. "Can you tell me anything about Tripp Willoughby? He would have just been brought in."

A nurse in aqua scrubs consulted her computer, then raised an eyebrow in Diana's direction. "Are you family?"

She couldn't lie. "No. But I'm a close friend. Please, anything—"

"I'm sorry. You'll have to wait until someone from his immediate family can answer your questions."

With a reluctant nod, Diana turned away and scanned the room for an empty seat. She found one facing the doors to the treatment rooms and plopped down, hugging her handbag to her chest. How long would it take before someone brought news? Would Brooke even remember Diana was there?

Before she'd finished the thought, the doors opened and Brooke appeared. Diana scrambled to her feet and rushed over. "How is he? What's happening?"

"They're prepping him for emergency surgery." Brooke grasped Diana's hand. "Come with me to the surgical floor waiting room. Dad's already gone up."

"Surgery?" As Brooke hurried them to the elevator, Diana tried to process everything. The only thing that made sense was a ruptured appendix. What else could cause such sudden, excruciating pain?

Brooke jabbed the button for the third floor. "If he wasn't already hurting so badly, I'd strangle him. I warned him several times this could happen if he didn't eat right and take better care of himself."

Recalling Tripp's recent stomach bug, Diana wondered now if it had actually been the early warning signs. "It's his appendix, right?"

"Appendix?" Brooke's mouth dropped open in an incredulous stare. Then, shoulders collapsing, she expelled a noisy breath. "He never told you, did he?"

"What? What didn't he tell me?"

The elevator doors opened at the third floor. Brooke draped her arm around Diana and marched her through the opening. "Girl, we need to sit down somewhere and have a long, long talk."

Had Tripp fallen into an echo chamber? Over the constant ringing in his ears, other sounds seemed amplified by a factor of ten. His eyelids felt like twenty-pound cement blocks. He tried to swallow, but his throat hurt like the worst case of strep ever.

"Tripp? You in there?" His sister's voice.

Little by little, he pried his eyes open, only to be blinded by a fluorescent light overhead. "Where—" It was all he could push past his raspy vocal chords.

"The hospital. You just had surgery for a blockage." Elbows braced on the side of the bed, Brooke hovered over him. "You could have died, you know. I'm half-tempted to kill you myself, you big, brainless—"

"Brooke." Their dad appeared at the bedside. "Enough."

Tripp couldn't think clearly enough to grasp why he was in so much trouble with his sister, so he decided this was a good time to drift back to sleep.

The next time he opened his eyes, the room lay in darkness. His whole body felt stiff and sore, but when he tried to shift his position, a twinge in his abdomen made him suck in a breath.

Oh, yeah. Surgery…blockage… It was coming back to him now, the recurring belly cramps over the past few weeks, the stabbing pain that grew steadily worse the day of Mom's funeral.

Mom's funeral. He sank into his pillow with a moan. The whole day had been one long, painful blur, both physically and emotionally.

And Diana. He remembered sitting next to her in the fellowship hall, right before he collapsed.

Great, just great. By now, Brooke would have told her everything. Tripp's best intentions of finally being honest with Diana about their breakup, of allowing her the chance to love him for who he was today—forever taken away from him by his own stubborn stupidity.

A brown-skinned man in scrubs pushed a rolling computer terminal into the room and switched on a muted light over the bed. His name tag read James Fessler, RN. "Doing okay, Mr. Willoughby? Any pain?"

Not the kind medicine could relieve. "Just a few twinges."

James checked Tripp's vitals, then changed out his IV bag. He handed Tripp a cord with a button on the end. "This will release pain meds. Don't worry, there's no chance of overdose. You want to stay on top of the pain so you can rest and heal."

"I know. I'm a veterinarian."

"Ah, so it's *Doctor* Willoughby. Where do you practice? I just got my kids a puppy."

"Not around here. In Juniper Bluff." For how much longer, Tripp wouldn't hazard a guess. The thought of facing Diana again terrified him.

"Over near Fredericksburg, right? Well, you get some rest, Doc. I'll check in on you later, but don't hesitate to buzz the desk if you need anything."

As soon as the nurse left, Tripp gave himself another dose of pain meds in hopes it would make him drowsy. Lying there in the dark with only his troubling thoughts to keep him company, sleep seemed his only escape.

A couple more doses got him through the night. About the time his breakfast tray was delivered, Brooke and Dad arrived.

"Wow. You look a hundred times better than when we left here last night." Brooke peeked beneath the metal lid on his tray. "Oh, joy. Broth and lime gelatin. No worries about me snitching a bite."

Dad circled to the opposite side of the bed. "How are you, son? You scared us silly."

"I'm okay. More worried about you." Tripp gripped his father's hand.

"Hangin' in there, best we can." Dad shared a glance with Brooke, who gave a quick nod, obviously some kind of private communication Tripp wasn't supposed to interpret. "I'm just gonna step out to the nurses' station and see if they have some coffee."

As the door closed behind his father, Tripp pinned his sister with a hard stare. "All right, what's going on?"

Arms crossed, Brooke plopped down on a chair. "Eat your breakfast and I'll tell you."

The beefy aroma of the broth was slightly nauseat-

ing, but if Tripp wanted to get stronger, he'd better try
to get it down. He took a few careful sips. While his
stomach settled, he glanced over at Brooke. "So...?"

"So...I'm pretty mad at you right now." She sat forward. "Do you have any idea what it was like for *me* to
have to explain to Diana about the Crohn's? Tripp, why
didn't you tell her?"

The broth churned through his insides. "I was waiting for the right time. And then—" He swallowed and
looked toward the window. "What Dad went through
with Mom, the thought of putting Diana through that—
I just couldn't do it."

"You big baby." Lips pursed, Brooke shook her head.
"She's in love with you, Tripp. Don't be an idiot. Don't
let her go again."

"You don't understand—"

"No, *you're* the one who's totally clueless." Rising,
Brooke approached the bed. "Just talk to her, Tripp.
Apologize and make things right, before it's too late.
She's in the waiting room right now. Let me go get
her—"

"No." Tripp's chest muscles clenched. He fought for
breath. "Not like this. Not while I'm lying in a hospital
bed with tubes in my arm."

Brooke glanced toward the door. When she faced
Tripp again, the frustration in her eyes had turned to
worry. "She's hurt and angry, Tripp, and she has every
right to be. If you don't reach her now, you may never
get another chance."

Long moments of indecision passed. Tripp's thoughts
sped through the uncertain future, and when he con-
templated facing it without Diana, his heart twisted.

The door whispered open, and Tripp jerked his head

toward the sound, both hoping and fearing he'd see Diana.

It was his father. Exhaling tiredly, Dad caught Brooke's eye and murmured, "I tried, but she wouldn't stay."

Only then did Tripp realize how ready he was to stuff all his fears about the future into a deep, dark hole and do whatever it took to convince Diana of his love. Ignoring the pang shooting through his surgical incision, he pushed himself upright in the bed. "What—she left already?"

"Sorry, son, but she was real upset." Hands stuffed in his pockets, Dad shuffled closer. "Said she only stopped by to make sure you were all right and had to get back to Juniper Bluff."

Brooke cast him a sad smile. "I'm sorry, Tripp. I tried to tell you."

"Not your fault." He looked away. "I brought this on myself."

Diana used almost an entire box of tissues during the drive home. Between the flood of her own tears and the spitting rain smearing the windshield, the road ahead was a misty blur, and she could only be thankful there hadn't been much traffic on a Tuesday.

Pulling into her garage, she shut off the engine and hammered the steering wheel with her fist. "How could you, Tripp?"

All those wasted years, simply because he was both too proud and too insecure to be truthful with her about his health condition. Did he have so little respect for her, so little trust in her love?

Now, how could she ever trust him again? Even if she

could forgive him—and she wanted to, desperately—
every time she replayed Brooke's description of Tripp's
battle with Crohn's, along with the potential complications she'd read about later on the internet, her thoughts
raced with the terrifying possibility that any future they
might hope for could be cruelly and painfully cut short.

It didn't matter how many sources quoted statistics indicating Crohn's was rarely fatal. What if Tripp
proved the exception? What if another episode like this
one—and Brooke had said it wasn't the first—turned
into something much worse?

She had to stop thinking about it before she drove
herself crazy. Hauling her travel bag from the trunk,
she entered through the kitchen door, only to be loudly
greeted by three howling cats and a squawking parakeet. Alice the rabbit was quiet, at least, hunkering near
her crate door and wiggling her nose.

"I missed you, too, guys. All right, all right, don't
trip me." Stepping gingerly around the cats, Diana made
her way to the bedroom and started unpacking. It was
still early. She could grab a bite of lunch and then relieve Kimberly at the doughnut shop.

Just keep busy. If she could focus on work and her
therapy pets group, maybe she'd get past the anger and
find a way to deal with the revelations of the last couple of days.

When Diana walked in the back door of the doughnut
shop an hour later, Kimberly looked up from her mix-
ing bowl with a start. "Didn't expect you back so soon."

"Nothing to keep me in Austin." Barely looking at
her assistant, Diana took an apron from a hook. "Who's
up front?"

"Nora. And don't have a conniption, okay? She, um,

had a little accident with the cappuccino machine this morning."

Good, a problem to deal with. Today, problems were Diana's friend. She started for the front before Kimberly could bombard her with questions about the trip. Or Tripp. She didn't want to talk about either one.

Avoidance worked fine for the rest of the day. And the day after that. And on into the weekend, at least until Sunday morning, when Doc Ingram caught her on her way into church.

"Awful thing about Tripp," he said. "First his mom dying, then him getting sick like that."

"Yes, awful." Diana offered a pinched smile. Out of politeness she asked, "How are things at the clinic? Are you managing okay?"

"Hasn't been easy. Good to know Tripp's on the mend. Can't wait to have him back." With a nod to his wife, waiting at the sanctuary doors, Doc Ingram excused himself. "You take care of that boy, you hear?"

"But I—" No use explaining. The vet was out of earshot anyway.

Then Marie Peterson arrived with her great-grandchildren, Seth Austin's kids, and bustled over to say hello. From Marie, Diana learned Brooke and Mr. Willoughby had driven Tripp home and were staying in one of the guest cabins.

Diana blinked. "He's back already?"

"You didn't know?" Marie's eyebrows bunched. "I just figured—I mean, I heard you two—"

The opening praise music began, saving Diana from an uncomfortable explanation. "We'd better go in to church."

She sidestepped into the pew alongside her parents

and grudgingly accepted her father's sympathetic one-arm hug. Dad's "Spidey sense" where Diana's boyfriend issues were concerned had kicked in big-time after she returned from Austin, and she hadn't been able to escape confiding the truth about Tripp and all that had happened.

"Heard he's back in town," Dad spoke close to her ear. "Planning on seeing him?"

Keeping her eyes on the song lyrics scrolling across the projection screen, Diana shook her head. "Still processing. Not to mention I've been busy getting organized for another therapy pets visit this afternoon."

"Sounds like an excuse to me."

Diana bit her tongue. "I—I just need more time."

And a whole lot more prayer.

From a cushioned chair in the cabin's sitting area, Tripp watched his sister puttering around in the kitchenette. "You really don't have to stay," he told her for the tenth time since they'd brought him home. "I can take care of myself."

"Uh-huh, like you've totally been doing lately." Crossing to his chair, Brooke handed him a plate of baked chicken breast and steamed green beans. Bland, but at least it wasn't hospital food.

"So I had a minor setback."

"Minor?" Hands on her hips, Brooke glared. "Have you forgotten you just had *major* surgery?"

"I've learned my lesson this time, I promise." Shifting to ease the strain on his healing incision, Tripp glanced over at his dad as he settled onto the sofa with his own plate of food. "How have you put up with this bossy kid for so long?"

"She's a handy little thing to have around." Dad cast his daughter a loving, misty-eyed smile. "Don't know what we'd have done without her this past year."

Tripp's first bite of chicken stuck in his throat. He forced it down with a gulp of iced tea. Dad was right, of course. Brooke was the glue keeping them all from falling apart.

Well, except for Tripp. He'd fallen apart mightily these past few weeks. But the pieces were coming together again, praise the Lord. Long talks with his father during his hospital stay and in the days since had helped him regain some perspective—about his mother's courageous battle with kidney disease, about the ups and downs of his own condition and especially about not letting fear of an unpredictable future rob him of happiness in the here and now.

But would Diana see it the same way? Would she give him another chance, first to explain and apologize, and then to try again to build a life together?

None of it would matter, though, if he didn't take his health more seriously. The obstruction was his own fault for ignoring the warning signs of an impending crisis. Now that he was thinking more clearly, he could see how his negligence had been a form of self-punishment for his "crime" of not being able to give his mother a kidney and save her life. As Brooke and his parents had been telling him for years, he needed to stop blaming himself for something that was never his fault.

When they'd finished supper and Brooke had washed the dishes, Tripp insisted she quit fussing over every little thing and sit down with him and Dad. "I'm serious," he said. "Brooke, you've got a job to get back to, so there's no point in y'all sticking around. I'll manage fine on my own. Besides, the Austins and Petersons are right next door, and Marie's already offered to bring meals over for the next few days."

"That's all well and good," Brooke said with a scowl. "What I really want to know is when and how you're going to start repairing the damage you've done with Diana."

Tripp matched her stare. "I fully intend to—or at least I plan to try. But not with my daddy and baby sister nagging me at every turn."

"Nagging? *That's* what you call making sure you don't ruin the rest of your life—or kill yourself in the process?"

The chinks in Brooke's armor were showing, and it saddened Tripp to realize he'd only added to her stress and strain. "I won't let that happen, sis. You have my word."

She sniffled and turned away, but not before Tripp caught her wiping away a tear.

"Brooke, my sweet girl," Dad said with a weary sigh, "it's time you took a rest from the caregiving. Let's do what Tripp says and get on home. Time we all got started on finding our way through this—" his voice wavered "—and on to whatever comes next." He pushed up from the sofa and patted Tripp on the shoulder. "Get a good night's sleep, son. We'll come say goodbye in the morning before we leave for the airport."

It was early yet, but as soon as his dad and sister returned to their guest cabin, Tripp crawled into bed. He'd been cleared for limited activity but had been up and around more today than he should have been. It just felt so good to be out of the hospital and back in his own place.

His own place—a rental cabin more suitable for a short-term stay than a permanent residence? He'd have to remedy that soon because he'd had plenty of time to think it over recently, and he felt more certain than ever that he wanted to settle down right here in Juniper Bluff.

And not just settle down but, Lord willing, make a home with the woman he loved.

Chapter Thirteen

Another week went by while Diana pretended everything was okay. Which wasn't easy when she jumped every time her cell phone rang, hoping and yet dreading she'd see Tripp's name and number on the display. He'd called three times already, but she hadn't been ready to talk. She hadn't even found the nerve to listen to his voice mails and had systematically deleted them. He probably figured she'd given up on him completely. If so, it served him right. Served them both right for believing in something they could never have.

On Saturday morning, as she mechanically filled customers' orders, Seth Austin walked in. Glad for the distraction of a good friend, she managed a weary smile. "Seth, hi. Haven't seen you in here on a Saturday in a long time."

"No Camp Serenity kids this weekend, and our only two guests are honeymooners." Seth's mouth quirked. "More interested in quiet walks around the lake than guided horseback rides."

"Ah." Diana glanced past Seth. "No Christina?"

"She'll be along. She's over at the drugstore refilling her prenatal vitamins."

"Won't be long now, huh?" An unexpected twinge of regret stabbed Diana's heart. The likelihood of her ever knowing the joy of having a family of her own had all but disappeared because she couldn't imagine it happening with anyone but Tripp. With a brisk inhalation, she shoved aside such futile thoughts. "So. What can I get you?"

"Regular coffee for me, extra strong. Christina asked for raspberry tea." Seth nodded toward the bakery case. "And a carrot muffin and cheese Danish."

"You two are so predictable." Smirking, Diana turned to fill Seth's order.

"Haven't seen you out at the ranch lately," Seth said as she set two mugs on the counter. One eyebrow slanted in an accusing frown. "This isn't like you, Diana. At least it didn't used to be."

Diana clamped her teeth together. "You know what it feels like to have your heart broken by someone you loved and trusted, so don't judge me."

"No judgment intended. Just an old friend who'd really like to see you happy with the man you love." Leaning closer, Seth braced his elbows on the counter and lowered his voice. "Look, with Tripp recuperating at his cabin, he and I have had plenty of time to get better acquainted, so I know all about the Crohn's and how it's the reason you two aren't together. I also know it's not like you to run from something just because it's a little scary."

"Isn't that exactly what Tripp did when he broke up with me in college?"

"For which he's paid dearly, sounds like to me. He's

crazy in love with you, Di, and the only reason he hasn't pushed harder to get in touch since he came home is because he understands you need time to come to terms with everything."

"Come to terms with the fact that he kept the truth from me all these years? That's going to take a while." Conscious of being in full view of her other customers, Diana swiveled sideways to swipe away an escaping tear. "Here comes Christina. I'll get those pastries for you."

She served Seth and Christina and was grateful neither said anything more on the subject of Tripp Willoughby.

She wasn't so fortunate when she stopped in to see Aunt Jennie later that afternoon. Her parents happened to be there, too, and their presence made it even harder to calmly justify why she'd avoided all contact with Tripp since he'd returned home.

"You need to settle this once and for all," her father said. "Either go patch things up or make a clean break. You owe that much to yourself and to Tripp."

Squashed between her parents on Aunt Jennie's love seat, Diana sat with her arms folded tightly against her chest. "I have no idea what I'd even say to him."

Aunt Jennie scoffed. "Words are highly overrated. Just go be with him, honey. God will take care of the rest."

While Diana shook her head and sniffed back a tear, her mother tugged her hand free and gave it a squeeze. "I have an idea," she said. "Let me call Tripp. I'll invite him over for Sunday dinner tomorrow—a gesture of kindness as he recuperates."

"I don't know, Mom…"

"Give this a chance, sweetie." Her mother kissed her cheek. "Your dad's right. This has to be settled, and you need to do it face-to-face."

An anguished sigh ripped through Diana's throat. "All right, but I should be the one to call him. And if Tripp agrees to come, no pressure, okay? Whatever happens, happens."

Her mother nodded. "Whatever happens, happens."

Steeling herself, Diana carried her phone out to the corridor. As she found Tripp's number in her contacts, a huge part of her hoped he wouldn't answer.

He did.

"Tripp, I, um…" She swallowed the nervous lump in her throat. "I wanted to find out how you're doing."

"Better, thanks." A kind of calm strength undergirded his reply. "Actually, I've been a lot more concerned about how *you're* doing."

She had no way to answer that without sounding cruel. "I'm coping," was all she said. "I know we need to deal with…everything. But you've just had major surgery, and I don't want to do anything to hinder your recovery."

"Diana, don't worry about that. I'm getting along fine."

"I'm sure you are. But—well, let me just get to the point. My mom would like you to come over for Sunday dinner tomorrow."

Tripp hesitated. "I hope this isn't strictly a pity invitation."

"No. Absolutely not." Diana marched to the end of the corridor. "Actually, I'm insulted that this is even an issue. That you would think so little of my family. Of *me*—"

"I don't." A sigh rasped through the phone. "That's a mistake I will never make again. Can we just chalk it up to pea-brained male pride?"

She scoffed. "Now *that* is a condition I definitely consider pitiable."

Another moment of silence elapsed. "Can we back up to the part where I said yes to your mom's invitation and let me add a simple thank-you?"

"That would be best. I'll text you directions to my parents' place."

"No need." His voice dropped to a nostalgic murmur. "I remember like it was yesterday."

Diana's throat clenched as she recalled the last time she'd brought Tripp home to spend a weekend at the ranch. She'd been so certain he was on the verge of proposing, and then he'd taken ill with what they'd all assumed was either a stomach bug or food poisoning. Tripp must not even have known about the Crohn's at that point. Then, only a few weeks later, she'd received the fateful phone call ending it all.

She cleared her throat. "So Mom usually serves dinner around one thirty. Come on over whenever you're ready."

"I'm looking forward to it…more than you know."

Diana wished she could say the same, but the mere thought of facing Tripp tied her insides in knots. "Okay, then. See you tomorrow."

"See you tomorrow."

When Tripp arrived at the Matthews ranch shortly after 1 p.m. on Sunday, Diana met him at the front door. The look on her face was anything but welcoming. In fact, she looked ready to bolt.

Mrs. Matthews rescued them both. She waved from the kitchen, a slotted spoon in her hand. "Come on in, Tripp. You can help Diana set the table while I dish up the veggies."

"Glad to, ma'am." Following Diana to the kitchen, Tripp cast a poignant glance toward the family's freshly cut Christmas tree, a sad reminder he'd never have another Christmas with his mom. "Thanks for having me over. It's really good to be here again."

With a kind smile that suggested she'd read his thoughts, Mrs. Matthews handed him a stack of plates. "You're welcome anytime, Tripp."

Diana barely looked at him as she gathered up napkins and flatware. "Dining room's this way."

"I remember."

The simple act of arranging place settings on the dining room table seemed to help Diana relax. When she reached past Tripp with a knife and spoon, she stood close enough that he caught the subtle fragrance of lavender.

To break the awkward silence, he asked, "How's it going with the therapy pets?"

"Pretty good. We visited the assisted-living center again last weekend."

Tripp released a gentle laugh. "I'll never forget the look on your great-aunt's face when she saw all those dogs for the first time. The therapy pets are going to be real blessings to all the residents."

"I hope so." Diana inhaled a shaky breath. "I should ask what else Mom needs help with. Dad's roasting chickens on the grill. Why don't you go ask when the meat will be ready?"

"Uh, okay. Sure." Tripp disguised a nervous gulp,

knowing if he really wanted to make up for lost time, convincing Diana's father of his honorable intentions was as good a place as any to begin.

Stepping onto the patio, he tried hard to keep his tone friendly and light. "Hey, Mr. Matthews, how's it going?"

"Thought I heard you drive up earlier." Diana's father opened the grill, releasing a burst of flavorful aromas that made Tripp's stomach growl in anticipation. "Chickens look done. Pass me that platter."

So Mr. Matthews wasn't in the mood for conversation, and Tripp couldn't help being relieved. The business of getting the meat to the table had saved them both from an uncomfortable father-to-hopefully-future-son-in-law interrogation. Tripp could wait for the next one until he'd actually slipped the engagement ring on Diana's finger—a day he prayed would be soon in coming. But first, he had to find a way to assure her he was in this for the long haul and would never let her down again.

The dinner was every bit as good as Tripp remembered from when he'd dated Diana in college. He appreciated Mrs. Matthews's frankness in questioning him about his dietary restrictions. Apparently, Diana had prepared her, because he could eat just about everything on the menu without hesitation, and he savored every bite.

Afterward, he offered to help with kitchen cleanup. Once all the leftovers had been put away, Mr. and Mrs. Matthews excused themselves to the family room, leaving Tripp and Diana with the dishes. The intimacy of working alongside her like this—Tripp rinsing plates and handing them to Diana to set in the dishwasher— brought back all kinds of pleasant memories from their college dating days, along with dreams of many similar days to come.

"This is nice," he murmured, his hand brushing hers.

"Mmm-hmm," she replied without looking up.

He handed her another plate but didn't let go. "Di," he said, waiting for her to meet his gaze. When she did, tension lines radiated from the corners of her eyes. With a tender smile, he reclaimed the plate and set it on the counter, then took both her hands in his. "This is the best day I've had in a long time. Please tell me there can be more."

Pulling away, Diana backed up a step and folded her arms. "What do you want me to say, Tripp? That all is forgiven and I'm fine with spending the rest of my life worrying about whether you'll end up in the hospital again? Or—or maybe even—"

The intensity of her response caught him off guard. Stunned, he reached out to enfold her against his chest, holding her close until she stopped resisting. "Yes, Crohn's can be a miserably annoying condition, and there are bound to be setbacks. But it's not a death sentence. I know what I need to do to keep it under control."

"I'm overreacting, I know." Slowly, hesitantly, her arms tightened around his torso. "I just can't lose you again."

The desperately sweet sound of those words wrapped around his heart and squeezed. "I'm not going anywhere." Cupping her cheek, he tilted her head and lowered his lips to hers in a kiss he hoped would convey the depth of his love and his enduring commitment to making a life with her. Ending the kiss, he smiled down at her. "Do you believe me now?"

Tears filled her eyes. "I want to, more than anything."

"Then take a leap of faith with me. Let's spend the rest of our lives making up for what we've been missing out on since I got stupid and scared and let you go."

"You make it sound so easy."

Tripp thumbed a droplet from her cheek. "It could be…if you'd let it."

She pulled out of his arms and turned away. "I don't know if I'm ready. I…I'm still sorting things out."

"I'll wait as long as it takes." Knowing there was nothing more he could say, Tripp slipped out. After offering Diana's parents his sincere thanks for dinner, he said goodbye.

As he drove down the lane toward the main road, an idea began to form. He just might know a way to convince Diana once and for all that he was here to stay.

Over the following week, Diana heard nothing from Tripp. Had she been too adamant about needing more time? If so, he'd taken her at her word, and she wasn't sure how she felt about that. Because the bald truth was she missed him. Missed him terribly.

Besides, after those moments of closeness they'd shared at her parents' last Sunday, she thought for sure he'd stop in or at least call. If they really did have hopes of restoring their relationship, a little more communication might be in order.

Where was he?

When he didn't show up for church Sunday morning, Diana's doubts increased. Catching Marie Peterson after worship, she nonchalantly asked about Tripp.

"Oh, far as I know, he's just fine." Marie glanced

around distractedly. "I know he's been busy catching up on work at the clinic. Also mentioned he had some business to attend to this weekend."

"Business? Like, out of town?"

"Could be." Waving at her husband, Bryan, across the foyer, Marie excused herself. "Got a roast in the oven, sweetie. Don't want to burn the house down."

"Of course. Don't let me keep you." Watching the plump woman hurry away, Diana had the distinct impression she'd just been given the brush-off.

Was Tripp keeping more secrets from her—and enlisting the aid of his landlady to cover for him? Diana did a slow boil as she marched out to her car. Apparently, the man had learned nothing about the cost of not being honest.

It wasn't until late Sunday afternoon that Tripp finally called.

"Where have you been all week?" Diana's effort to keep the peevishness out of her tone had failed.

"Busy with patients, mostly. And I'm still supposed to be taking it easy, so lots of naps and early bedtimes."

Slightly mollified, she drew her lower lip between her teeth. "Well, it's good to know you're taking care of yourself."

"I really want to see you, though. Any chance you're free for dinner tonight?"

Tiger crawled into Diana's lap, circled three times, then plopped down and began purring. "Well, I don't know," she grumbled, stroking the big cat's head. "I might have had a better offer by now."

"Rain check, then?" The flippant tone of his voice infuriated her. "Give me a buzz when you're free."

"Tripp Willoughby! I'm sitting here on my sofa in

ratty sweats, and you should know perfectly well I have no better plans than microwaving leftovers and dining with three cats, a rabbit and a parakeet."

"So can I pick you up in an hour?"

If not for yearning so badly to see him, she'd give him an earful about his presumptuous attitude and then hang up. "Okay, fine. But only because it'll be a lot more satisfying to chew you out in person for ignoring me for an entire week."

He chuckled softly. "If you still feel like that two hours from now, I will humbly oblige."

Two hours from now? What could he possibly have up his sleeve? With a gruff goodbye, Diana nudged the cat off her lap and went to change into clean jeans and a sweater. After freshening her makeup, she tried three different hairstyles before settling on wearing it loose. She spent another ten minutes deciding whether to wear her new brown boots with the legs of her jeans tucked inside or pulled down over the top. Tucked inside won out. She decided it made her look more assertive—and where Tripp was concerned, she needed every ounce of fortitude she could muster.

She'd just given the pets their supper when the doorbell rang. Drawing several long, slow breaths, she took her time in answering. Tripp had made her wait for an entire week. He could stand to cool his heels on her front porch for a couple of minutes.

When she opened the door to his apologetic grin as he clutched a bouquet of fragrant flowers in bright, Christmasy colors, her resolve crumbled. "For me?" she asked, and then wanted to kick herself for sounding like a simpering female.

"No," he replied with a completely straight face, "I

brought them for Alice. Thought she'd like munching on them."

Diana's mouth fell open. "Tripp—"

"I'm serious." He pointed at the various flowers in the bouquet. "Daisies, roses, pansies—rabbits love these. And I checked with the florist. No harmful chemicals."

"Um, okay…" Brows in a twist, Diana reached for the bouquet.

He didn't let go. His grin returned, while his eyes softened into a look that weakened her knees. "I'm kidding. These are totally for you."

"Ever the practical joker, aren't you?" With a quick shake of her head, Diana seized the flowers and spun on her boot heel before Tripp could notice the effect he was having on her. "Come on in. I need to find a vase."

Once she'd placed the flowers in water and set the vase on the kitchen table, she retrieved her purse and jacket. "So. Where are we having dinner?"

"We'll get to that." Tripp paused on the front step while she locked her door. "There's one stop I want to make on the way."

Diana didn't have much choice except to go along with whatever Tripp had planned. She sat stiffly in the passenger seat of his SUV and tried not to be obvious as she noted the route he took. After reaching Main Street, instead of heading downtown or toward the highway to Fredericksburg, he wound through another residential area.

Finally, her curiosity got the best of her. "I don't know of any restaurants around here. Care to clue me in?"

At that moment, Tripp pulled up in front of a ranch-style brick house with a white porch rail. The house looked empty, and a For Sale sign stood near the curbside mailbox. Tripp shut off the engine and pushed open his door. He cast Diana an enticing smile. "I've got the key. Want to go inside and look around?"

She glanced from Tripp to the sign and back again. "You're buying a house?"

"The owners accepted my offer on Friday."

"You're *buying* a house."

"I think you just said that." Rolling his eyes, Tripp stepped from the car. He strode around to Diana's side and helped her to the curb. "The place is structurally sound, but the interior needs updating. I was hoping you could help me with some ideas."

Still in disbelief, Diana stumbled along beside him as he strode up the front walk. "*This* is what you've been doing all week between patients and naps—house hunting? But Marie Peterson gave me the impression you had business out of town."

Glancing her way, he wiggled his brows. "Oh, so you cared enough to ask about me?"

"Has anyone ever told you how infuriating you can be?"

"You. Several times."

"Well, it's no compliment. Seriously." As they reached the porch, she set her hand on his arm. "Why the sudden rush to buy a house?"

He pulled a key from his pocket, then turned to her with another of those beguiling smiles, this one fraught with meaning. "Because Juniper Bluff is my home now, and I decided it was time for more permanent living arrangements. This town has everything—absolutely *everything*—I've ever wanted in life."

Diana's breath grew shallow. "Tripp, I—I can't—"

"Just come in and tell me what you think." He un-locked the door and pushed it open. "Our dinner reser-vations are at six, so we don't have much time."

Speechless, Diana followed him through the empty, echoing rooms as he flipped light switches and pointed out various features. It was a nicely arranged house, with small formal areas, a den with a stone fireplace, an eat-in kitchen and three spacious bedrooms. Diana had to agree, though—updates were in order, especially in the straight-from-the-'70s kitchen.

"By the way, I *was* out of town this weekend," Tripp confessed. "The owners have agreed to let me move in now and rent until closing, so I drove over to Austin to arrange to get my apartment furnishings out of storage."

"Oh. That's nice." Between the swiftness of Tripp's decision and the reasons he'd given her, Diana felt like she was still playing catch-up.

The den faced the rear of the house. Tugging on a cord, Tripp drew open the dingy, olive-green drapes covering a sliding patio door. "Nice backyard, don't you think?"

Diana fanned away a cloud of dust emanating from the drapes before peering through the glass. "Wow, it's big. A privacy fence, too."

"Yeah, I thought it would be great for a dog or two… and maybe kids someday."

The implications of this show-and-tell grew clearer by the moment. "Last time I checked, you didn't have a dog. As for kids, I didn't think… I mean, after what Brooke told me while you were in surgery…"

Tripp fingered a lock of hair falling across Diana's shoulder. "What exactly did she say?"

She couldn't look at him. "That you were scared of having children because they might inherit the propensity for developing Crohn's."

"It's true, I let the possibility worry me for a long time." Breathing out softly, he rested his arms across her shoulders and dipped his head until their foreheads touched. "But I had some long talks with my mom during her last days, and then with Dad after my surgery, and it finally sank in that spending my life with the woman I love outweighs every problem we could ever face."

Emotion tightened Diana's throat. "When you got sick at the funeral—when I thought I might lose you—" Her eyes pressed shut, she shook her head. "If that happened to one of our children—"

"*If*, Diana, not when. Genetic predisposition is just a percentage number, not an absolute. And remember, we've got God on our side. He's carried us this far, hasn't He?" Tilting her chin, he kissed the tip of her nose. "I want a family, Di. I want it more than I ever dreamed possible. And I want it with you."

Pulse thundering, Diana wrapped her arms around him and held on tight. "I never, ever stopped loving you."

"Then you have to believe as I've come to accept, that God brought us back together because we were never meant to be apart." Easing from her embrace, Tripp drew something sparkly from his breast pocket, then took her left hand in his.

She gasped. "Is that…a *ring*?"

"I've been holding on to this for twelve long years."

"You mean—"

"I bought it just a few days before my first serious

hospital stay, before I learned I had Crohn's." Tripp's eyes darkened. His voice grew thick. "When I called you to break up, I was clutching this ring against my heart. I'd convinced myself I had to let you go, but I was never able to part with this one tiny symbol of hope."

"Oh, Tripp." Scarcely feeling the tears slipping down her face, she cupped his cheek. "If only you'd trusted me. If only you'd trusted our love."

"It's a mistake I'll never make again. I can't undo the past, but if you'll have me, we can start right now working on the future we always dreamed of." Still holding her hand, he sank to one knee. "Marry me, Diana. Let's not waste another minute."

Sinking down next to him, she threw her arms around his neck. "Yes, Tripp Willoughby, I will marry you—and the sooner, the better!"

Epilogue

One month later

Making a rush trip to the ER was *not* the way Tripp envisioned spending his wedding day. At least this time it was for a much happier occasion than dealing with his personal health issues. Seemed Diana's matron of honor, Christina Austin, insisted on going into labor three weeks early—and two hours before Tripp and Diana were supposed to say their "I do's."

"Honey, sit down." Diana looped her arm around his waist. "Wearing a groove in the waiting room carpet isn't helping Christina and Seth in the delivery room."

"Maybe not, but it makes me feel like I'm doing *something*." Tripp snuggled Diana under his chin. His stomach was in knots, and it had nothing to do with the Crohn's. He couldn't help imagining both the terror and the elation of someday being with Diana for the birth of their own child.

Except there needed to be a wedding first, and the whole day had just been turned upside down.

A sudden commotion drew his attention to the door.

The widest grin Tripp had ever seen split Seth's face. Wearing a blue paper gown over the dress pants and shirt he would have worn to the wedding, he strode into the waiting room. "Jacob and Elisabeth Austin have officially arrived!"

A collective whoop of joy filled the room. Bryan and Marie Peterson rushed over with Seth's older kids, Joseph and Eva. All four of them smothered Seth with laughter and hugs, while Diana squeezed Tripp until he almost couldn't breathe. Eyes filling, he hugged her back. He'd calmly delivered any number of puppies and kittens during his years as a vet, but this was an entirely different kind of thrill—and it wasn't even his baby.

Diana tugged on his arm. "Let's congratulate the new dad."

Joining Seth and his family, Tripp and Diana listened as Seth recited the statistics. "Jacob weighs five pounds, nine ounces, and Elisabeth is five pounds, two and a half ounces. And they both have healthy sets of lungs!"

"How's Christina?" Diana asked.

"Tired, but so, so happy." Seth still hadn't stopped grinning.

Tripp pumped Seth's hand. "You look like you could use some rest, yourself, *Daddy*."

Eyes widening, Seth palmed his forehead. "Aw, man—your wedding!"

"Hey, no worries. We'll just reschedule." Although delaying making Diana his wife was the very *last* thing Tripp wanted to do.

Diana stretched up to give Seth a kiss on the cheek. "We should go. Give Christina our love, and tell her we'll see her soon."

"I will. And thanks for being here." Seth winked.

"Once y'all tie the knot, I'll be happy to return the favor someday."

After a round of goodbyes to Seth and his family, Tripp escorted Diana down to the parking lot. The January day had grown blustery as the sun sank toward the western hills, and Diana minced along in spiky heels, a short jacket and the shimmery waltz-length white dress Tripp wasn't supposed to see until she started down the aisle at Shepherd of the Hills Community Church.

She did look amazingly beautiful, though, and Tripp told her so for probably the twentieth time that day as he helped her into his SUV.

"At least my dress is bought and paid for," she said. "Your rental tux is due back tomorrow."

With a tight-lipped nod, Tripp closed her door, then dashed around to climb in behind the wheel. He sat there for a minute while his thoughts raced. "What if… what if we go over to the church right now and have Pastor Terry marry us in a private ceremony?"

Diana stared at him, her brows forming a V. "Are you serious?"

"Never more so." He shifted to face her. "Unless you'd be too disappointed not to have your big church wedding?"

She lifted her hand to his cheek and lightly kissed his lips. "The wedding isn't nearly as important to me as spending the rest of my life as Mrs. Dr. Tripp Willoughby."

"Then…"

Facing forward, Diana snapped on her seat belt. "Let's do it."

* * *

When they arrived back at the church, Diana spotted her parents' car outside the fellowship hall and figured they had stayed to pack up the reception food and decorations.

"That looks like Brooke's rental car, too," Tripp said.

"Great, they're all here. I'll go tell them the plan while you track down Pastor Terry." With a quick kiss, Diana shoved open her door.

Hurrying into the fellowship hall, she shouted, "Mom, Dad, everybody! The wedding's still on."

"What?" Brooke whirled around and nearly toppled a floral arrangement. "I thought you'd decided to postpone."

Diana's mother rushed out of the kitchen. "Everyone's already gone home, honey. And the food's all packed for freezing."

"None of that matters." Diana took Brooke's hand on one side and her mother's on the other, then smiled toward her father and future father-in-law as the men strode over. "Our families are here, and Tripp's rounding up Pastor Terry. We'll save the food and hold a reception in a week or two, after we get back from the honeymoon."

"I'm so glad," Brooke said, beaming. "I didn't know how I'd get time off work again so I could make the trip to be your bridesmaid."

The door flew open and Tripp marched in, the pastor in tow. He swooped Diana into a hug. "Let's get married!"

"Wait," Diana burst out. "There's still one person missing. Aunt Jennie will be so disappointed if she misses my wedding."

Mom shook her head. "We took her back to her apartment hours ago. I'm not sure she's up for another outing so soon."

"Then let's take the wedding to her." Diana looked to Pastor Terry for confirmation.

He nodded in agreement. "I'll call the administrator right now and explain what's happening."

Tripp pulled Diana aside. "With this last-minute change of plans, I've got something else I need to take care of. I'll meet you at the center in a few minutes, okay?"

Arching a brow, Diana straightened the boutonnière pinned to his lapel. "Might this have anything to do with a surprise wedding gift?"

"It might." He winked. "You'll have to wait and see."

Already feeling as if her heart would float right out of her chest, Diana did her best to contain her curiosity.

By the time everyone arrived at the assisted-living center, an aide had brought Aunt Jennie to the community room. A few other residents had also gathered, which was fine with Diana since she'd gotten to know them during the regular therapy pet visits. They seemed almost as excited as Aunt Jennie to be able to attend Diana's wedding.

Even some of the staff looked on as Diana and Tripp recited their vows. Following the brief ceremony, the family joined Aunt Jennie in the dining room for the evening meal. Diana's mother had brought the wedding cake, and everyone applauded as Diana and Tripp fed each other the first few bites from the upper tier, specially made with Crohn's-friendly ingredients. Afterward, the staff served generous slices to the residents.

As they sat around the table finishing their cake and

sipping decaf, Tripp leaned close to kiss Diana's cheek. "Be right back, okay? By the way, this would be a good time to invite everybody back to the community room."

"Tripp...what are you up to?"

His only reply was a mischievous grin.

A few minutes later, with Aunt Jennie settled in a comfortable chair and other residents filtering in from the dining room, Diana glanced toward the foyer to see Kelly Nesbit, Vince and Janice Mussell, and a few other therapy pet volunteers with their dogs. Before Diana could gather her wits to ask what was going on, the grinning volunteers paraded into the community room. One by one, they peeled off to stop and say hello to the elderly residents, who were delighted by the unexpected visit.

Then Tripp entered, a perky tan-and-white corgi prancing alongside him. He and the dog headed straight for Aunt Jennie. Yipping with excitement, Ginger danced on her hind legs as she stretched up to shower Aunt Jennie with doggie kisses.

"Oh, my Ginger! My sweet little Ginger-dog!" Tears streamed down Aunt Jennie's face as she cuddled the companion she'd missed so much.

Dumbfounded, and loving this man more than ever, Diana captured Tripp's hand. "When did you do this?"

"I made a quick trip to see Mrs. Doudtman in San Antonio few days ago. Kelly's been keeping Ginger for me until I could spring the surprise." He slid his arm around Diana and tilted her chin for a kiss. "We can always use another therapy pet, right? Besides, I told you when I bought the house that it had a great yard for dogs."

"Yes, I do seem to remember that. I just hope Ginger will make up quickly with my menagerie."

"Mrs. Doudtman said she adapted very well to both her shelties and a cat she adopted recently. Her grand-kids, too, so I'm not anticipating any problems."

"Good." Diana squeezed in closer. "Because I also remember you said something about having kids of our own someday."

"Speaking of which…" Passing the leash to Diana's father, Tripp nudged her toward the exit. "What do you say we get started on our honeymoon, Mrs. Willoughby?"

"Why, Dr. Willoughby, I thought you'd never ask!"

* * * * *

If you loved this tale of sweet romance,
pick up these other stories
from author Myra Johnson

RANCHER FOR THE HOLIDAYS
HER HILL COUNTRY COWBOY

Available now from Love Inspired!

Find more great reads at www.LoveInspired.com

Dear Reader,

I hope you enjoyed this visit to Juniper Bluff in the Texas Hill Country as much as I did. Not long after Diana Matthews first appeared as a supporting character in *Her Hill Country Cowboy*, I knew I needed to write her story. A hardworking small-town business owner, still single after all these years? Must have been some heartbreak in her past. That gave me the idea for a reunion story, and into my plot walked Tripp Willoughby.

After Tripp ended their college romance, Diana spent years struggling with doubts, confusion and resentment. Can you relate to her fears of opening her heart again? Can you identify with Tripp's fears about the future, his need to spare the woman he loves from the possibly life-altering complications of his health condition?

Fear is a powerful motivator, but often the things we're most afraid of are only vague uncertainties, events that may never come to pass. If we truly trust God, though, those fears don't have to rule our lives. Scripture tells us, "There is no fear in love; but perfect love casteth out fear" (1 John 4:18a). So if fear is holding you back from something potentially good in your life, try courageously stepping out in the full assurance of God's perfect love. Even if things don't turn out as hoped, it doesn't mean God has abandoned you. We can't see the bigger picture, but God can. Just keep trusting and praying for His purposes to unfold in your life.

Thank you for joining me for Tripp and Diana's story. I love to hear from readers, so please contact me through my website, www.MyraJohnson.com, or write to me c/o Love Inspired Books, Harlequin Enterprises, 233 Broadway, Suite 1001, New York, NY 10279.

With blessings and gratitude,
Myra

COMING NEXT MONTH FROM
Love Inspired®

Available February 20, 2018

AN UNEXPECTED AMISH ROMANCE
The Amish Bachelors • by Patricia Davids

Mourning a broken engagement, Helen Zook flees to Bowman's Crossing. There she finds herself clashing with her new boss, Mark Bowman. Sparks fly. But with Mark soon returning to his hometown, is there any chance at a future together?

COURTING THE AMISH DOCTOR
Prodigal Daughters • by Mary Davis

Single doctor Kathleen Yoder returns to her Amish community knowing acceptance of her profession won't come easy—but at least she has the charming Noah Lambright on her side. Even as Kathleen comes to depend on Noah's support, she knows an Amish husband would never accept a doctor wife. Could Noah be the exception?

A FAMILY FOR EASTER
Rescue River • by Lee Tobin McClain

When Fiona Farmingham offers to rent her carriage house to single dad Eduardo Delgado after a fire at his home, he accepts. Having failed his deceased wife, he plans to keep their relationship strictly professional. But six rambunctious kids, one wily dog and Fiona's kind heart soon have him falling for the pretty widow.

HER ALASKAN COWBOY
Alaskan Grooms • by Belle Calhoune

Honor Prescott is shocked former sweetheart Joshua Ransom is back in Love, Alaska—and that he's selling his grandfather's ranch to a developer! As a wildlife conservationist, Honor is determined to stop that sale. But when the secret behind Joshua's departure is revealed, can she prevent herself from falling for the Alaskan cowboy once again?

FINALLY A BRIDE
Willow's Haven • by Renee Andrews

Disappointed by love, veterinarian Haley Calhoun decides her practice and her Adopt-an-Animal program are enough. Until she discovers the handsome widower who showed up at her clinic with an orphaned boy and his puppy will be her point of contact for the adoption program. Will working together give both of them a second chance at forever?

THEIR SECRET BABY BOND
Family Blessings • by Stephanie Dees

Mom-to-be Wynn Sheehan left her dream job in Washington, DC, after her heart was broken. When she becomes the caregiver for Latham Grant's grandfather, she's drawn once again to her long-ago boyfriend. But with her life now in shambles, is her happily-ever-after out of reach for good?

———————

Get 2 Free Books,

Plus 2 Free Gifts—

just for trying the Reader Service!

Mark Bowman lifted his straw hat off his face and sat
up with a disgruntled sigh. Trying to sleep on a bus was
hard enough, but the sound of muffled weeping coming
from the seat behind him was making it impossible.
He turned to look over his shoulder. The culprit was
an Amish woman with her face buried in a large white
handkerchief. She was alone.

"*Frauline*, are you all right?"

She glanced up and then turned her face to the window.
"I'm fine."

It was dark outside. There was nothing to see except
the occasional lights from the farms they passed. She
dabbed her eyes and sniffled. She was a lovely woman.
Her pale blond hair was tucked neatly beneath a gauzy,
heart-shaped white *kapp*. He didn't recognize the style
and wondered where she was from. "You don't sound
fine."

"Maybe not yet, but I will be."

The defiance in her tone took him by surprise and
reminded him of his six-year-old sister when she didn't
get her way. Experience had taught him the best way to

stop his sister's tears was to distract her. "I don't care much for bus rides. Makes me queasy in the stomach. How about you?"

"It doesn't bother me."

"Where are you headed?"

"To visit family." The woman's clipped reply said she wasn't interested in talking about it. He should have let it go at that, but he didn't.

"Then someone in your family must be ill. Or perhaps you are on your way to a funeral."

She frowned at him. "Why do you say that?"

"It's a reasonable assumption. You'd hardly be crying if you were on your way to a wedding."

Tears welled up in her eyes and spilled down her cheeks. With a strangled cry, she scrambled out of her seat and moved to one at the rear of the bus, effectively ending their conversation.

Confused, he stared at her. Somehow he'd made things worse, and he had no idea what he'd said that upset her so. He shook his head in bewilderment.

Don't miss
AN UNEXPECTED AMISH ROMANCE
by Patricia Davids,
available March 2018 wherever
Love Inspired® books and ebooks are sold.

www.LoveInspired.com

Looking for inspiration in tales
of hope, faith and heartfelt romance?

Check out **Love Inspired**® and
Love Inspired® **Suspense** books!

New books available every month!

CONNECT WITH US AT:

Harlequin.com/Community

Facebook.com/HarlequinBooks

Twitter.com/HarlequinBooks

Instagram.com/HarlequinBooks

Pinterest.com/HarlequinBooks

ReaderService.com

LIGENRE2018

Inspirational Romance to
Warm Your Heart and Soul

Join our social communities to connect with other readers who share your love!

Sign up for the Love Inspired newsletter at **www.LoveInspired.com** to be the first to find out about upcoming titles, special promotions and exclusive content.

CONNECT WITH US AT:

Harlequin.com/Community

 Facebook.com/LoveInspiredBooks

 Twitter.com/LoveInspiredBks

LISOCIAL2017